DEAD MEN NAKED

DARIO CANNIZZARO

ISBN: 9781521103630

Any resemblance to persons living, dead, or undead, is probably explained by the philosophical concept of Synchronicity, but should not be forcibly inferred.

To my father,
who went away hugging the ghosts of the people he loved.

O Lord, give each person his own personal death.
A thing that moves out of the same life he lived,
In which he had love, and intelligence, and trouble.

Rainer Maria Rilke

The spirits of the dead continue to exist in the unseen world which is everywhere about us; and they all become gods of varying character and degrees of influence.

Hirata

My first name, Angelene.
The prettiest mess you've ever seen.

PJ Harvey, Angelene

one

There are no secrets to the dead, as after this life they still exist, and known to them is the exit from this stage of fools. Alas, everyone will join in this secret eventually, in his own personal way; but a great death takes a life of preparation. That is why it is said that in the final moment you get the chance to review your entire life, to watch it unfold before your eyes as you're turning your soul in.

But while everyone can picture a last moment of intimacy with his or her demise, very few stop and think of the end during all the other moments of their life. If Death itself was a person, we would have noticed his or her presence long before the last check out. Bumped into him on the subway. Exchanged a seat on a plane. Or glanced over at his watch to check what time it is because you're running late.

We purposely relegate this thought to the very end — an end that's simply pushed to the back of our mind and only rarely comes back, usually in the heart of the night, haunting our sleep. That's why, even if Death were an actual person, we'd never recognize him.

The personification of our Death.

Even if he turned out to be your pale, skinny neighbor upstairs.

Every good story has its beginning in the middle of the action, so I'll spare you the boring details of my anonymous life until that dreadful night. I'll give you the basics: I'm twenty-eight, an only child, parents long dead. I'm smart enough to finish college *cum laude*, but not smart enough to pick something actually useful. Poetry. What was I thinking again? But that's a different topic. Of course, as no good story ever started with Once upon I time I was drinking a cranberry juice, I'll start with me and Neil — my best friend Neil, who knew the secrets of my buttery heart that trembled and fell in love too easily; Neil, whose heart was lighter than mine — Neil and I, as this story starts, in a pub at sundown in the City. Nameless voices filling the air and the smell of alcohol and sweat and people trying to find shelter from themselves. That night saw us celebrating my third month unemployed. But the important part of the conversation, the part that set everything in motion, came unnoticed when we ended up talking about my new neighbor, the guy in the attic. We didn't know his name, and we didn't care – having surrendered our lucidity to the spirits already, we were wildly speculating about pale Skinny Guy, so Neil said,

He's a vampire, I tell you.

No, Neil, he's not. Vampires don't exist.

Have you ever seen him in broad daylight?

I couldn't say that I have.

Does he freak out in front of a cross? Garlic?

Never shared a meal; never been in his house, my friend. How would I know?

The conversation weighed the possible pros and cons of having a vampire living in the attic above my old apartment and involved a good number of tequila shots with beer backs. As we'll discover, the effects of tequila on human beings are heavily underrated. But let's stick with the order of events. Neil kept insisting on his vampire theory and said,

So, let me recap: He always dresses in black. He's pale as the moon and so tall and thin it's a friggin' miracle he can even stand up straight. If he's not a vampire, then he's definitely something. Possibly a Satanist. Does he wear t-shirts with goats on them?

I wouldn't know, Neil. I saw him once—twice. Never even said hello to him.

And he moved in what, three weeks ago?

More or less. More tequila?

We drank to a point where we couldn't keep the conversation going logically anymore. We paid, left the tip, and then decided to call it a night. My house was close by so we walked in that direction. Neil took a rounded piece of metal out of his pocket, with a little chain attached to an end. An old watch. He started spinning it around until the chain would grip around his hand, only to proceed to spin it in the other direction to release the chain – in, then out, then in again, then out - a manual and imprecise pendulum.

You still have that old thing? I asked.

It's my grandfather's, you know. Besides, it's just for looks, he said, spinning the time away from his hand.

In the night-cold air we let the drinks take over and instead of saying Goodbye, Good night, Neil suddenly jumped ahead and started running up the old stairs of the house, skipping my floor and heading for the attic.

Neil! Where the hell are you going? Neil! You'll get us in trouble! I said, hoping that my whispers weren't actually shouts, mislead by the alcohol in my blood.

If he sleeps in a coffin, we oughta kill him! Said Neil, and continued, I just wanna check out his place. Lights are out. He's probably out.

It's one thing to discuss the weird guy in the attic that you don't know and make fun of, but it's entirely another to break into his house. Right? Try reasoning when drunk and tell me how it worked out for you. So instead of trying to force him down and Go home and See you tomorrow, what did I do? I followed him up to the attic, to the door of Skinny Guy. The doors that are doomed to open are always unlocked, and this was one of them. We were in.

As soon as we closed the door behind us it was dark, and I immediately sensed a stench. Mold and dust and rot. I imagined nests of rats and evil things crawling in the dark – not a good thought to have. I was holding Neil by the shirt like a child. We stood there, frozen, until our eyes were able to see. Dark wooden floor, old unpainted plaster walls, a rusty stove, and nothing more, other than a feeling of restlessness. I wanted to say Let's get out of here, but I didn't have time as Neil walked towards the window. Before I could get to him I heard him scream. It was a short-lived scream that died in his throat as he fell. I jumped to help him, shouting Neil! and when I moved closer - there it was.

Blocking the window was a dark silhouette, black melting with the surrounding black, a mantle and a hood, darkness taking shape, and as the streetlight shone on a long blade I fell down and hurt my face, on the ground, helpless. I tried to move towards the wall to find something to grip onto and pull myself up, but before turning to check on Neil again I heard voices that said,

Does he *actually* see you?

I do not know. It seems so. The other one?

He is grasping at the wall.

One of the voices was difficult to identify—it could have been the voice of a little girl or an old man or a young woman or a toddler muttering *mamamama* for the first time. The second voice was clearly one of a heavy smoker – words shaving his throat out and trembling. I finally managed to pull myself up and leant against the wall to keep myself straight.

I finally took a clear look.

The *smoker* was a six-foot-tall giant black bird. Black like oil, black against the hooded tall figure on his right. The blade the tall guy had in his skeletal hands was to my knowledge a scythe. My heart paused for a second, only to catch the energy needed to start racing faster and faster, and so I had to hold onto the wall, while with my foot I reached out to Neil to poke him and wake him up. The two figures started to talk again,

They see us, mate – *rasping voice of hell talking* - that is rather strange to me, and I don't even think entirely possible. If not out of place completely.

I know. The other one saw me already, I would dare say.

The tall figure removed his hood, revealing the face of my neighbor - Skinny Guy. At this particular point, I wasn't sure if I could cross off *vampire* from the list, but seeing his face was enough to help my heart slow down. As logic seeped in, I thought that maybe he was one of those guys that dress up as knights and myths and demigods - for deep is the human longing to mimic the immortals.

A man in his right mind would simply collect his passed-out friend, ask for forgiveness, and go on with his life. But I wasn't in my right mind. See, alcohol is not a friend, it's not the solution to your problem, it's not a balsam that when passed on your mind cleanses it from pain. It is a drug and a demon and limbo and dark oblivion. But I didn't know that then, and as I was possessed by this demon - which has a sense of humour of its own - instead of going about my own business I shouted,

Nevermore!

So the giant bird turned towards me and said something like Oh, very very smart; nice. I'll make you meet the dead fella in a heartbeat!

He spread his arms, or wings. The costume was really good; all looked real, dark wings five feet out from each side. I was starting to feel my heart pounding again when Skinny Guy stopped him and said,

Leave him alone.

What?

Leave him. He saw me anyway, and he is still here.

What about his dead friend here then? I can't just leave him here?

Things have a way of figuring themselves out.

Great night out, my friend. Remind me not to hang with you anymore.

Still holding tight to whatever was on the wall behind me, I muttered something like,

Sorry, guys. Look, my friend isn't dead; he's just passed out. He does this when we drink too much—I kept poking Neil with my foot—so if you'll excuse us for our disturbance, we actually just hit the wrong floor. Our night's over, but you can go on to whatever party you were going to. Great costumes, by the way.

The crow hopped towards me and I pressed myself closer to the wall as he was really pretty scary. He turned my friend's body over with his long, black beak.

Dead, he said.

Blood was coming out of Neil's nostrils and his face was distorted and his eyes were wide open. Unnaturally open, unblinking. Whatever was holding me up wasn't enough anymore and I fell to my knees with my hands over my mouth and my heart racing the final mile up to my throat. The voices of the bird and Skinny Guy became murmurs too heavy to be whispers, but needles stinging in my ears together with a buzzing sound. And I wasn't listening anymore, but rather throwing my eyes at Neil's body - at the window - at the two guys - at his body again - and the blood and the buzzing became unbearable and then I believe I saw Neil standing *outside* of his body and looking at his body; and there were two of him and then the ringing sound became a flash of light in my eyes and my body gave up and I saw *darkness there, and nothing more.*

I'm in a cold room with a strange smell. Old air and dust. No one had been here for a while. There's light coming in from a big window. It's a bedroom, but it isn't mine and I can't see anything I recognize. When I move my feet they bring with them a black sticky substance. I look at the floor and it's dark. Dark and glossy and crawling. The light beaming onto it makes it shimmer in hundreds of little flashes of light. I take another step and realize that the floor is liquid. And I am able to walk on the dark liquid without being swallowed.

I take two, three steps towards the window and I see a shadow there. Against the window, where the light is, there is a tall Being of Beauty.

The light isn't coming from the window but from the person standing against it. And the person is a woman and there's warmth, a wave of happiness coming from her. I can't see her face clearly.

Her dress is covering her whole body and it's white. It looks like a cape or a robe, and I want to go nearer and see her face. Her hands are resting on her belly and she has her head tilted to the right. I think she's looking at me but I can't be sure. The light becomes more intense and it's like every particle of it is touching my skin and making it new and it's a mystical experience.

All I want to do is go near her and touch her because I know that if I touch her I'll be saved. But I stay here, still, floating on the liquid floor, looking at this light-emitting figure and now I see her face.

And it is the face that Beauty wears when it doesn't want to hide in flesh and bones. It is beauty and love and compassion and in the secrets of my soul I'll always know splendor visited me that night.

And the floor now starts to take me down into it but I'm not scared because she's smiling at me, and the last thing I see is her silhouette against a beam of light and her smile and her eyes like shooting stars and forgetting all this I wake up.

two

Spinning in the darkness behind my eyelids. A carousel of dark filaments all around. I opened one eye for a second — morning, and I was in my bed — and then closed it again because the outside world was spinning, too. One by one pieces of my body started to call themselves out. Cold feet, check. Cold legs, check. *What time did I get home?*, my brain told me, while checking off the list. Cold arms, check. *Am I sleeping in the same t-shirt I had on yesterday?* Mouth opening and closing, dry and with a terrible—unbearable—flavor of nicotine and vodka and, *is that tequila?* A gag rose and I was ready to puke. Don't move. Don't move. Yet. Minute by minute the spinning got easier to bear, adjusted to the pace of a sloppy merry-go-round, dancing still to the rhythm of a thousand hammers banging on my head.

I managed to open both of my eyes and the pace of the room slowed until the world just gently circled around me. I managed to sit on the side of the bed and grab a sweater, put it on, a pair of pants, put them on, no socks, and walked to the kitchen counter — *What did I do last night?* — turned on the coffee machine — *Was I with Neil? Yes, I was* — filled the metal cup with coffee grind — *Did we get that drunk?* — placed it in the arm and closed it and pressed the button.

The loud noise coming from the machine had the effect of a kick to my ear and I let out a little howl and stopped the machine immediately - but then pressed the button again because coffee is your only true friend the morning after a bender of this magnitude.

I was dazed. Last night, last night. *What the hell happened last night?* Me and Neil in a bar drinking tequila, talking about. About, about. About? I stopped and put two spoons of brown sugar in a cup and poured the black coffee and stirred while trying to recall what we'd done. Hung on the counter with a hot cup in my hand I scanned the room to check for signs, for clues. The room was clean and empty, filled only with the unpleasant smell of someone who'd drunk too much and hadn't showered. *Shower, that's good*, I thought.

I sipped some of the coffee, left the cup on the counter, and moved towards the dresser, took a pair of underpants and black socks and a pair of jeans here and a plain t-shirt there and dragged myself to the bathroom, massaging my right temple in a ritualistic circular movement to beg the Gods of the Hangover for sympathy. I have to call Neil, I thought, while opening the bathroom door, instantly recoiling from the foul smell of day-old digested tequila, and I almost fell face down, but instinctively knelt to puke someplace safe and that's when I saw Neil - and the memories came back like flashes. Me and Neil leaving the bar. Me and Neil going to the attic and something wasn't right and his face was deformed and his nose was bleeding and he wouldn't wake up and the Skinny Guy said something and I passed out, and now I was puking on Neil's body, with the same deformed face but a whiter shade of pale on his face. I tried to keep myself straight with one hand and to shake him with the other, and when I stopped retching I started shouting Neil! Wake up, Neil, you son of a bitch! And I was shaking him and then I was shaking him harder, with both hands, but my brain wanted to stop because it was useless.

Neil was dead.

But my hands and my eyes didn't believe it so they kept shaking his body and my mouth had no more words to say but Neil, Neil, Neil, caught in a loop of disbelief and I started slapping his face because I was enraged, because I hated him, because I hated that he was dead and I was there, helpless, shaking a dead body, calling his name, until my mouth surrendered to the fact that Neil was dead and stopped calling his name, and the hands started believing it too and stopped, and I fell back, sitting on the floor with my face covered in blood and vomit and snot and tears, next to his dead body in my bathtub.

I sat there crying with a blank mind for I don't know how long. Eventually I found the strength to stand up, helping myself up with the side of the tub, careful to avoid looking at what was in there. I made my way to the sink and had to fight my gag reflex back. I turned on the cold water and splashed it on my face first, then when my face was clean I got rid of my t-shirt and splashed water on my body, and then soap, and then cold water again, and if I could have rained cold water and soap in my eyes and in my mind to clean up what I saw I would have done it. But the stains on the soul can't be washed away with ease. I started crying again, face in the sink, water running, alone. Neil. My best friend Neil, my childhood friend Neil - dead. Dead like anyone can be, a dead body in the bathtub in my apartment. I threw more cold water over my face and left the room, leaving everything as it was: dirty and foul, like every death is, every time it knocks on your door. What happened in the attic? How did we get back here? My mind was trying to make sense of it all, working backwards to find out why and when and how, so I closed the bathroom door and moved to the kitchen. I needed more coffee.

What happened last night?

While the coffee machine was still buzzing, I called the emergency services and said there was a body in my apartment. They asked me if the body was definitely dead and if I knew him and I replied Yes and they told me not to move, not to go away, took my address and dispatched someone, and I didn't move, and I didn't go away, but stood still, leaning against my counter with my cup of coffee, waiting for someone to knock at my door and tell me it was just a bad dream.

When the policemen arrived — four or five of them — three came in and asked Where's the body and I showed them, pointing at the bathroom door with my arm extended and a full cup of cold coffee and then I placed the cup in the sink and asked Do you want a coffee? but they didn't reply and I just stood there. A policeman with a shield and classic pants and a black sweater and brown shoes came closer and asked What's your name, and Did you find the body—Yes, I did find the body; he's my friend, Neil, my voice said. And then he made me sit down and he opened a little notebook and started asking me questions like what did I do last night and how would I describe my relationship with the victim, and while he was talking and asking questions the two other men disappeared into the bathroom and eventually when they came out other men came in, and my house was full of strangers and a dead body—Neil's dead body—and dreadful smells and for every question the man asked me I had other questions bouncing around in the back of my mind, so I asked,

Could I have been drugged?

Why do you think you've been drugged?

I don't know. I've never had such a hard time remembering what happened just the day before.

Alcohol can do that to you. Do you — did you and your friend drink a lot? Drugs?

No, no. No drugs. We drink when we're out, you know, for fun. I don't know if it's a lot.

Why do you think you've been drugged, he insisted.

Because I have weird memories, strange flashes. Like hallucinations. From last night, I said, recalling that something was off. Then I continued, You should check the attic.

Why should we check the attic?

Because I think Neil died there.

The police officer looked at the bathroom door, then at me. And why do you think that?

Because I remember him falling down in the hallway, while going up in the attic.

Okay. Why were you going to the attic?

We were in the attic because we were drunk, and we skipped my floor, and we found ourselves up there.

And how did the body end up in the bathtub?

I don't know. Maybe - I stopped. Was it like that? Now I remembered Skinny Guy in his costume. The officer must have noticed my face, my reaction to something, because he asked What? What is it?

I know! I almost shouted, then continued, We went up the stairs and Neil and I bumped into the guy that lives there, a very tall man, very, very skinny. He was dressed up in a black robe or something. We wanted to check him out because we thought he was a Satanist or something and we walked up there and-

A Satanist? So you went up to the attic with a motive?

No, I mean, yes, we just wanted to talk to him, you know? And we were drunk and we didn't stop to plan it or anything. We went upstairs and he was dressed in a black robe and had a blade—a blade! Did he kill Neil? It must have been him. It was dark and I couldn't see properly or don't remember, but I saw Neil falling down. Then I passed out and they must have carried us down here. You should check the attic! I shouted.

They?

Yeah, there were two of them, one dressed up as a bird, a crow. A giant black crow, with a rasping voice. It was well-acted; gave me chills down my back.

So let me get this straight, the officer said, You and your friend broke in to your neighbor's house late last night. Drunk. He had company, a giant bird—and I am quoting you here, he said, while giving me a suspicious look — a giant black bird and your neighbor; what's his name?

I don't know his name.

A giant black bird - quotation marks - and your neighbor, whose name you don't know, who was in possession of a blade. And your friend died upstairs, you say? And you woke up here and found him here?

Yes. Yes, I think. It's hard to recall.

I crossed my arms and felt like the chair was eating me. The officer scrolled through his notebook. It was obvious from his face that he didn't believe me. We sat at the table, in silence, for a good five minutes.

Eventually Neil wasn't in the bathroom anymore; he was brought out in a plastic bag while the two guys that came out of the bathroom gave a sign to the officer that was questioning me, and he jotted down something quickly and then told me,

Apparently your friend doesn't show any external signs that can give us a probable cause of death. We'll need an autopsy. And we need you to come with us, to make sure you are alright.

But I am alright.

We have to check. It's procedure. Until we know what happened to you and your friend, we must be cautious. I'll check the bar you mentioned and the attic, and we'll keep your neighbor for questioning as well. But you have to follow us.

I didn't do anything.

I believe you. But you have to come anyway. He said this and closed the notebook and said, Put on some clothes.

I was still shirtless, with only a blanket over my naked shoulders and wet pants from all the water I'd spilled. While the police were still in the apartment I went into autopilot mode and took some pants and a t-shirt and socks and underwear again, hitting restart on the day clock, and got dressed. From the door I heard the police guys calling the radio saying they had a probable fifty-one-fifty or something and another number and other police talking. I went out of the room and finally asked,

Officer, am I being detained?

Detective, please. No, you just have to come with us, and we'll check you're okay.

I left my house in a police car; people were staring from their windows, and neighbors were playing hide and seek behind their doors, carefully left unlatched — but no sign of any skinny man, let alone a giant bird.

I met Neil about twenty years ago. Our families had both moved to the City from different places. We weren't anything like the local children - we had no past there, only future; we naturally bonded. What often happens when you meet a childhood friend is that you share an abundance of First Times — first kisses, first joints, first jobs — and it's usually on those first times that relationships thrive. Maybe that's why you'll never forget your first love.

I bet you'll never forget your first real friend, and for me that was Neil — my first true friend and probably the only one. What also often happens is that life throws innumerable curveballs at you and you find yourself moving houses and moving cities and moving countries, or you simply grow apart because the new first times you're looking for are different from the ones your old-best-friend is looking for. Neil and I were lucky enough to grow over our differences, and to be there for each other when needed. So when my dad died too early and my mom followed him because she was beautiful and fragile and beautiful, because saying beautiful once can't really do her justice; when I lost my parents I was old enough to live by myself, but not old enough to deal with those things alone, Neil was there for me. Even when his parents moved back because life gave them the chance, he stayed.

We have — *had* — our differences, but we always stuck together, understood each other, and never really judged each other, which is much more than you can usually ask from most relationships.

He was never scared of diving in and talking to a girl for me. He'd help me overcome my stupid shyness, my refusal to act on my life and take the world in my hands; and we spent countless Friday evenings together, talking, drinking, and hanging out. We'd meet every Saturday morning at a diner to have breakfast, or skip weeks altogether because our latest crush was demanding all our attention. It didn't matter, we'd always come back to each other like it had only been a day.

And now that link had broken, that chain made rotten – now the future got to its tail, and only past was left for me and Neil.

The specials on the menu this particular Saturday morning were autopsy for Neil and psychiatric evaluation for me. I wasn't crazy, but simply hungover and paranoid, and Neil wasn't murdered, but dead from a heart attack. If you ask me how it's possible to die from a heart attack at that early age, I'd probably mutter something involving a giant bird. Which didn't exist. Nor did Skinny Guy. The officer — detective, sorry — who questioned me came back to inform me that no one had ever lived in the attic, as it's not suitable, as I'd probably witnessed myself. Still not certain about what happened, I asked,

So how come there was a guy there?

Probably was just hanging out there illegally or, from what you've described, maybe pursuing some kinky stuff. Whatever you saw, there's no evidence of it.

Are you sure I'm not crazy or, at least, soon-to-be-crazy?

I'm not, but the doc is. Did he give you anything?

Pills. To sleep.

Good. Sleep is what you need.

I went home. The funeral was set in Neil's hometown, two days later. I didn't shower, brush my teeth, or set foot in the bathroom that day, but laid on my bed for an endless time, looking at the ceiling, and I wasn't even sad, I didn't feel anything, my body was as numb as my mind, and the only thing I could think was that damned phrase from that old poem, *Whom the gods love die young.*

So I took my pills and forgot myself into darkness.

three

My head wasn't spinning and that was a good change. I opened my eyes. Kitchen counter, couch, TV set, clothes lying around. I'd left the window ajar and a cold morning breeze was coming in. *I should stop sleeping dressed and wear pajamas*, I thought. I sat on the edge of the bed. Everything looked normal. Peaceful. What did I expect? A bleaker color, a shade of darkness all around? Trumpets and violins following my steps?

The world doesn't care.

I *did* care though. And even if objects kept their normal shape and color and smell, my perception of them didn't. I hated all of it. I couldn't stand the look of the room, of the bathroom door. I needed to get out. So I took some clothes and threw them in a duffel bag and some clean shirts and a suit and the keys for the car and the pills for sleep and closed the door behind me. On my way out of the building, people whose faces I'd seen before stopped me to ask Are you okay? and What happened? and I didn't really want to talk about it. I didn't want to think about it. I didn't want to think about Neil. About death. But that's just the inevitable thought, and once you let it in, it will never disappear. So when I reached my car, I had to fight tears back, because that car wasn't just mine, it was mine and Neil's. We bought her, a black '57 Chevy, because we thought modern cars were devoid of a soul, and we needed something special for our rides. This black, old, rusty girl was our mechanical baby, one we promised to care for, and if possible, keep alive forever. And forever it will stay alive for Neil.

So I got into the car and started driving. I drove out on one road and merged on to another and I hated all the cars and all the people. I finally got to the road where everything around it is flat and I started driving south. I knew where I was headed. Neil's hometown. It took me the whole morning to get there and that was a good thing. I paid attention to the road and to stupid songs so I didn't have to pay attention to the thoughts in my head.

In Neil's hometown I found a hotel with vacancies available and decided to check in. I grabbed a sandwich and a soda from the vending machines and holed up in my room with the TV on and my brain off. All afternoon I had the urge to open a can of beer or to drink a shot of something, anything. I fought the urge until willpower wasn't enough – so I took the car and drove, without looking right or left or up or down but just straight in front of me until the sun was down and it was night again, and finally I decided that it was the right place and time and I parked and let myself go into a bar.

The place was crowded with people and I liked it. I was able to fill my head with other voices and to melt unnoticed in this sea of humanity. I waved to the bartender and ordered a beer which was gone too soon so I asked for another one. Two swigs later the beer was done and my mind felt able to deal with itself. All the thoughts I'd managed to keep out were given permission to come in and I decided I needed another beer to hear all of them out. Halfway through I switched to double whiskey, neat. I raised the glass to Neil and sipped. With the side of my eye I caught someone giggling at my gesture, so I turned.

She was leaning on the counter with a tumbler glass in her hand. And the first thing I noticed were her blue, blue eyes, because the blue sucked everything into them, like a coin thrown into a lake. Her blonde hair was tied up in a casual bun like she didn't really care that people were around; this carelessness didn't diminish the effect of her beauty on me. When I kept my eyes on hers for too long without noticing doing so and without saying a word, she smiled. And I felt a little warmth reaching out to my cheeks and smiled back. And with the smile, she came closer, and unaware of the battle I was fighting inside – each of ourselves has one - she asked,

Are you okay?

Hi. Yes. Thanks. You?

I am.

Great, I said, and moved the glass towards hers to toast.

What are we celebrating?

It's a toast. To Neil.

To Neil, she replied while our glasses tinged. And who's that?

My best friend.

I see. You here with him?

I'm here *for* him, I said, and then regretted it, and quickly asked What's your name?

Mallory. Mal. It's nice to meet you, she said and sipped from her glass.

Louis. Pleasure to meet you, Mal. We shook hands. Do you want a drink? I asked.

Oh, thank you, but I don't let strangers buy me drinks in a bar.

You don't?

No. I buy drinks for them, she said while waving for the bartender.

The guy behind the counter leaned in to hear Mal's voice asking for two shots of tequila. The glasses arrived and we smiled at each other and drank them down in one shot. She gestured to the bartender *Two more* and I felt, again, on the road to a hangover and Neil was still alive like a voice in my brain telling me to ask her to go, to move to someplace quiet.

We should go somewhere. Someplace quiet, she said.

You're reading my mind, I replied, and stood up. Where are we going then?

To my house.

To your house?

Yes. Don't you wanna to go someplace quiet? My house is. And I got drinks.

I smiled.

What? she asked.

Well, that was quick.

Don't. I like you, but not that much.

I'm not complaining.

Unless you have to go meet that Neil of yours.

No, I'm – I paused, then said, I'm going to check on him tomorrow.

Good.

We left the bar and Mal opened her car door and gestured for me to go with her. I told her I'd follow in mine. She gave the car a nasty look, but nodded and started her engine.

She slid easily out of town and drove south for a couple of miles and the houses became dark shadows, far apart. All around I could glimpse only the horizon and small trees and eventually we got to her house and it was around dinnertime but we weren't hungry for food. The first thing Mal did when she got inside was to grab a bottle of tequila. The second thing she did was dig in a cupboard to find two packs of peanuts and a bag of expired chips which we ate anyway while drinking tequila from big glasses.

We spent the whole time on a washed-out red couch next to a black coffee table with empty glasses on it. I was selfish and impolite and blind to the situation and didn't ask Mallory a single question - I was just talking and talking and talking, like the dam of my inside river was broken and all the water started rushing downhill, outside where people are, so you just close your eyes and cross your fingers and hope no one will get hurt.

But I wasn't really telling her anything about myself. Because that's what we do, what we learned to do. We put on masks and behave according to what's accepted. So I wasn't free to say things like I've just witnessed my best friend dying with my own eyes, or Have you ever seen a giant bird, or I am afraid of death and scared I'm going to be lost forever and there's nothing I can do. No. I was smiling and drinking and avoiding showing myself, my true self, all while filling the air with mindless comments out of the textbook about life, the universe, and everything else. Life according to Lou, unemployed and alone.

But suddenly something ticked inside and a thought popped in my head, and I heard it coming in Neil's voice, something like Stop talking, ask her what she does, you dumb-dumb. So I did and she replied,

I study, she said.

College?

Psychology, that's it.

Interesting. Is it your second degree?

Why my second degree?

I assumed you'd already be out of college. Sorry.

You assumed right, but it's a very big field of study. You can't imagine how many things you have to learn before you can call yourself a professional.

I didn't mean to offend you.

You didn't.

Okay.

Okay.

We sat in silence now and the couch seemed as big as the room. *I broke it*, I thought. *I broke the spell.* I sipped another bit of tequila and again my brain spoke to me in Neil's voice saying *You should kiss her*, and she was looking at me with her big blue eyes and the neck of her t-shirt was too large and kept falling down and she kept pulling it up and moving her eyes from the bottle to the glass to me and when she did look at me she smiled and I imagined what Neil's face would have looked like if I told him that I was with a beautiful woman drinking in her apartment and I didn't kiss her and it was like I was seeing him making Go for it gestures. And I turned my head towards Mal and came just a bit closer but really it was just to grab the bottle on the other side. But instead she kissed me.

She kissed *me*.

I kept my eyes closed and moved my arms around her and it was sweet and wet and fast and I opened my eyes for a split second and Neil was smiling at me and I closed them again and lost myself into that kiss and...

Neil was *where*?

I opened my eyes again and yes, Neil was standing there, behind Mal, with a smirk on his face. I jumped back and yelled and slapped my hands over my mouth. Mal's eyes went icy and cold and distant and she just stared at me. I felt hazy but managed to hold it together and, not looking at where I believed I saw Neil, I poured more tequila into my glass until the bottle was almost empty and then took a mouthful from the bottle before picking up the glass. Without looking at her I said,

I'm sorry.

You should be.

I know.

That was the worst kiss ever.

I know.

Have you ever done this before?

What? Of course I have! I said, raising my voice. Of course I have, I repeated, more calmly.

Yeah. Yeah. Of course. And do you usually jump backwards and scream?

I drank and without looking up I replied No.

No. Great. So only with me then.

No. I mean yes. I mean it never happened before. But.

But what?

It's nothing, I must just be stressed out.

Usually these things relieve stress, y'know.

I know. But tomorrow.

She didn't say anything.

Tomorrow, I said, I have to bury my best friend. Neil.

Oh.

Yes.

I'm sorry.

I'm sure you are.

No, I'm sorry if I made fun of you. It's hard losing people. Letting them go.

Yeah, I guess.

It is.

We sat there, Mal holding my hands in hers. I slowly regained the courage to look around. No Neil. I'd made a fool of myself and blown my night with a beautiful girl thanks to my brain projecting things. And what kind of man was I anyway, hooking up with a stranger the day before my best friend's funeral? And crying in front of said stranger, whose hands were warm and I wished I could wrap them around my heart, which didn't have a way to cry but could turn my chest into a cold lake of emptiness. I turned my face down, and muttered,

He's gone.

He is.

I'll never see him again.

You don't know that, she said, and started stroking my hair.

What do you mean? He's *gone*.

Yeah, but you don't know you're not gonna see him anymore.

I turned my head up and she kissed me again. And then, in silence and like a sacred ritual, she stood, still holding my hand, and led me from the room.

I'm in a hotel room and I'm alone even though I feel like someone was here with me. I look around and see two double beds. I need to take my car to go someplace, but the keys are missing. I go outside and there's a crowd of people looking at me and as soon as they see me they start laughing, mocking me. I hide in the room again and now two people are sleeping in the beds. I try to wake one of them up, but I couldn't do it. I don't know who they are.

The crowd has gone so I can take a walk outside because there is someplace important I need to go even though I don't know where. I open the door and start walking.

I stumble upon two identical trees. One of the trees bears fruit and blossoms while the other is bare and skeletal. Uncared for. Unloved. I pick some fruit from the blossoming tree and am about to bite it when a cawing catches my attention and I see a little crow. The crow speaks and I know it has Neil's voice even though all I can hear are caws. So I tell him I don't understand, and he spreads his wings and flies away and the sky becomes darker like its feathers until it is night. I circle back and the road brings me again to the door of the hotel.

I can see the shapes of the sleeping people's bodies underneath the blankets. And they are the shapes of women.

I look closely and I see myself reflected, like in a mirror, and when I uncover the first body it is naked and pale and voluptuous.

Mallory. And the other body is now floating in the air and every move one makes is reflected by the other, like they were one. I hear the now-familiar voice, the one I heard the night Neil died, saying Wake up.

four

The room was dark. Only silence and unknown smells. Mallory's. I was at her place. Without moving my head, I stretched out my arm and reached for her side of the bed. The hand lingered on the ghost shape of her body, now only a cold and empty spot. I lay silently in the bed listening for noises, for signs of her presence, for anything I could process to tell me this wasn't a dream. Something to tell me that bad nights are just one in a million, that *tequila nights* don't kill people. A sign of ordinary life. What time was it? I was late. Late for the funeral. I picked up my clothes and scanned the room to check if I forgot anything, then moved again into the living room—it was bigger and brighter than I recalled, and the only pieces of furniture—the couch aside—were a small, yellowish table with three chairs in different colors, a rocking chair covered with clothes, and two bookshelves filled with books, some of which looked really old. Probably her study books, I thought, and went to the counter that divided the room from the kitchen and looked for a piece of paper. I found a notebook and opened it and ripped out the last page and then I looked for a pen. I found one on the small refrigerator—had to scribble on the side of the page to make the pen work again—and left a note saying *At the funeral. Call me later,* and my telephone number. It felt good doing it. The banal repetition of everyday events seemed a ritual to me. Something ancient and common, but special. It made me forget, at least for a moment, about what the day had ready for me. But then thoughts of death and sorrow came back, melting my chest into a lake again.

The morning air was nice and fresh and for a moment I thought of walking to the hotel. But the roads going back were made for metallic chariots and the sun was a menace that would have burnt my body and my thoughts. I looked around to see if Mal's car was there, but the driveway was empty. I suddenly realized that I didn't even try to clean myself after the night. Lost in my animal instinct, I cherished the smell of a night of victory. But some smells need to remain secret; I was wearing yesterday's clothes and my breath was foul. I needed to get changed before sliding through unknown people. Another mask to hide behind.

I drove back to the hotel with the windows rolled down, letting the dry air come in and out, hoping to keep my mind fresh. I arrived at the hotel, and once in my room I started grabbing clothes from my bag. I undressed slowly, left my dirty clothes in shapeless piles on the floor and tiptoed into the bathroom. The water I let run on me was holy, washing away my sins; in the morning light reflecting from the tiles I felt blessed. I kissed the water like it was alive, let it into me, and came out into the world anew.

When I finally gave the room a last scan before going, I noticed a minibar. I corrugated my face – I swear this was not here before, or I would have stayed in the room. I caressed the top of it, a pagan altar with peanut offerings to the Gods of Oblivion. I opened its door with respect; two water bottles claimed the central space, while crowding the door with their shimmering reflections were cheap alcohol nips. But there I caught it; in the very far corner, shining above its lesser peers, a mirror image of the golden calf that threw the people of Moses into despair – Jose Cuervo Especial, my tequila, my love.

Without giving importance to the gesture, I took the small bottle and hid it in the side pocket of my jacket. For comfort and sustainment, my mind thought. I put on my new shoes and a new face, tied the laces and closed my soul to my eyes, and was ready to go say farewell to my best friend.

The cemetery was small and peaceful and not far from the hotel, just beyond the main street. Neil's was not the only funeral of the day—every death is unique, yet death is everywhere, everyday. I saw Neil's picture on a big board and walked directly there with my sunglasses on. I recognized his parents, but they didn't see me, blind in their sorrow, eyes on the closed casket and ears tuned to the useless voice of the priest. There were enough people, my mind thought. Enough to show that during your stay here you were loved, and this felt somehow important to me. My hand instinctively checked the little bottle of tequila in my pocket and unscrewed the cap. When the ceremony started I managed to keep on the edge, and with all the eyes on Neil, I secretly hit the bottle once. The comfort that kiss provided! I sipped another bit, and thanks to the residual alcohol of the night before I was already getting a buzz. The words of the eulogy slipped without sense around my head, as I didn't care what Neil was for others; I knew what he was for me and I needed no other words.

I missed him.

I missed him in my bones and in my gut. It was a physical feeling, a ghostly limbic resonance with something that wasn't there anymore. And while I was quietly, gently, intimately weeping, I felt a presence, someone next to me. I turned my head just the slightest bit to catch him with the corner of my eye, and there I saw him.

Neil.

I felt a weight on my shoulders like someone just climbed onto my back and my face felt cold as the blood drained away from it and my knees started shaking and I struggled to keep myself from fainting, in front of me there he was; I was looking at my friend—the same man who was dead in the casket and dead in a plastic bag and dead in my bathtub—I was looking at that same man standing there, and I saw him opening his mouth in a smile, and my brain said,

Neil!

Everyone turned to look at me because that wasn't a thought but my voice, loud and clear, almost a scream, slinging *Neil!* from the back of the crowd. I called his name out at the exact moment that my knees gave up their battle with gravity and my arms moved to my face to get rid of the million black butterflies that started crowding my view.

And like a house of cards I fell, all pieces down.

My nose tingled and I felt a sharp pain in my head and when my eyes were strong enough to open again I found myself sitting on the grass with my back to a tree and the crowd that had been looking at the casket with Neil inside was now turned to me. The new attraction of the day. Neil, I thought, and said it faintly, Neil, and people started chattering and I heard ownerless voices saying Give him space, let him breathe. I tried to stand up, but someone held me down for a second and said Easy, boy and I recognized Neil's father and hugged him like he was mine.

- A father lost early, a father never owned -

and

I was a little kid and I started crying - on the outside this time, and another ownerless voice said It's hard when you lose your friends; and the voices asked me Do you remember what happened and I didn't say that I fainted because I saw a *ghost*—that's what you call it when you see someone who's dead, but you see him anyway standing next to you—I didn't say that, but I just kept weeping and hugging Neil's father, and he patted me on the back and shushed and told me that everything would be okay.

I wanted to believe him.

We shuffled to the house for the buffet and my little tequila bottle was already empty and the euphoria it gave me was already gone. I didn't want to think about what had just happened, and every now and then my eyes would meet Neil's father's ones and he would look at me and smile with half his mouth – a smirk of comprehension, a glimpse of connection, an invisible link made of sorrow – and blink or raise a glass from far away as though we were sharing a secret, the tie that is feeling the same emotions for the same people, the gripping hand of fire in your gut which is empathy.

I reached out to where the alcohol was but I saw no tequila, and maybe that was a good thing, so with fear in my heart—fear of having more *hallucinations*—I got some champagne and poured it and drank it down and then I drank more of it and red wine and a couple of whiskeys. People around were doing the same, drinking and eating in the postmortem ritual. Because that's what you do when something you can't explain happens, you hide in the rituals and make them yours. And eating is survival, is a direct connection to the fact that yes - we're alive. Fuck death, we're alive. So everything I was eating and everything the other people were eating wasn't just food but *everything else*. We were eating the sorrow away and claiming our lives back. And everyone around was serenading the parents who'd lost a child, so I managed to go unnoticed for a while, until I ended up in a corner, with a glass in my hand and Neil's uncles around me recalling those times and these other times and I was empty and far and hollow and when I looked around the room it wasn't to wave hello to the living but on lookout for the dead.

I was the last one to go. I hugged Neil's dad a bit more and kissed his mom goodbye. Neil was very much like his mom. Blonde and always smiling. With good eyes. The eyes you want to see when something bad happens. I scanned hers for a moment too long, and both pairs, mine and hers, filled up with salty water, so I rushed myself away, because sometimes when it's too much you run away – trying only to run away from yourself. I was tipsy from the alcohol and glad I could walk back to the hotel to get my things and check out and then drive, drive back home.

As I entered the room I saw a shadow running across the window and I kept my hand on the door handle to sustain me, and I said to the empty room *Neil?* and when, after a couple of seconds, I had no answer and no more shadows in my eyes I laughed at myself, but it was a nervous laughter because I wasn't expecting silence like a normal person – I craved an answer to my question. So now in the empty room I finally asked myself, *What the hell happened at the funeral?* and tried to make sense of it. But the only sense was that I saw a ghost, or believed that I saw one, and then I thought that I probably saw him because I wanted to, so maybe I was being crazy. Or drunk. Maybe I was drunk. I wasn't. A bit on the edge, yes, and alcohol is the most common poison that helps you mess with perception, so maybe I projected Neil there because I was drinking. But now I'd had more to drink than this morning and I wasn't seeing any ghost. Maybe I was just stressed out and I was thinking all this while sliding out of my pants and my shirt and throwing the shoes and the rolled-up clothes into the bag. And I sat on the edge of the bed almost ready to go, but looked around the room again just to be sure. But the truth is I wanted to see him. If there was even a slight chance that my friend was still there, as a ghost, as anything, I wanted to see him. Because death puts the burden of letting go on whoever stays alive.

But I saw nothing, and the alcohol was slowly vanishing, so I blamed the tequila.

The tequila.

I drank tequila the night Neil died. And saw him as a spirit, or ghost, or whatever you call whatever he was. I drank tequila yesterday, and this morning, and I saw him again. Both times. Was it something about tequila? Was it possible that, with a bit of it, gates opened to unknown worlds? And why was I even having such crazy thoughts?

I turned to the bag and checked that everything was packed. I opened the window to let some real air in and those thoughts out. I don't know how long I sat there, looking out.

Just as I was ready to close the door on everything and everyone and go back to my life, my phone buzzed. A name appeared on the display, a name I hadn't saved, so with an awkward feeling I answered,

Hello?

Hey, stranger. Are you still in town?

Mallory.

five

Some people come into your life because destiny brings them, and when they've served their purpose, life gets rid of them. I thought Mallory would have been just the warm consolation of a night, that I'd never see her again, so when I spoke to her on the phone, I felt like I was speaking to something already over. I mumbled too many words in between the important ones, but agreed to see her. Normality seeped in again, the unavoidable swings of the uncaring world. When she arrived at my hotel, we started walking with no particular place to go. Silence for a few steps, and then she asked,

How was the funeral?

It was alright.

Many people?

Enough. Just enough.

Did you know his family? You said you were close.

Yes. His father is a nice guy.

I bet he is.

Yes.

You happy I saved my number in your phone for you?

Oh. Yes, yes.

She walked quietly on my right. Every three steps or so we'd look at each other and smile. When I said I was going to miss Neil, she smiled and took my hand. I smiled back and closed mine on hers, like I would do with a long-time lover. Our two souls touched between our fingers, and we kept walking with no destination.

He'll always be with you, you know, she said.

I laughed. Yes, I think so. I—*should I tell her*, I thought?—I had a hallucination today; I kind of saw him. At the funeral. I said it and regretted it.

She didn't even flinch and said, You saw him?

Kind of. Yes. I think I saw him, but then I passed out. Maybe it was the stress, I don't know.

Do you believe in an afterlife?

I don't know. Maybe.

I do. But I don't believe it's a reward or a punishment. I just believe the spirit carries on.

That's a comforting thought to have.

It might very well be terrible.

Why?

Where does the spirit carry on? she said, with a rapid, almost angry movement of her hands.

I don't know.

What if it just stays here and goes nowhere. Unable to interact. Just window-shopping at life through a dirty glass.

I looked at her in silence.

What if the spirit, the soul, stays here?

I kept silent.

What if it haunts you?

Like in a movie? I replied.

No, I'm talking real life. What if you really *did* see your best friend? What if his spirit wants to communicate with you?

What did you just say?

What if your best friend's ghost is near you. All the time. Even now.

Even now, I said, and looked around. *Nothing.* I continued, Then I hope it's a good thing.

Tell him.

What?

Tell him.

Tell him what?

That it's a good thing.

A good thing?

To be here, she said. To still be here. Even after.

I opened my mouth in disbelief. *Is she crazy?* I thought, followed by *Am I crazy?* I did see, or believed I saw Neil's ghost earlier today. I did feel like he was talking to me the first night I met Mallory. I felt like he wasn't far from me. But that was crazy. I wasn't ready to do such things. Talking to dead people. Facing the unknown.

I believe you, she went on. I believe you when you say you saw your friend. I think you actually did.

Oh, okay. Thanks for that.

Did you hear me? I'm serious. I believe you.

I don't know. I don't believe in ghosts.

You should.

I should. And why should I?

Because he's right here, right now.

Yes, in spirit and whatnot.

No. His ghost. He's next to you, she said, pointing to my left side.

I turned and looked at the empty space next to me. No one there. I looked at her again. I felt my face losing its color again.

That's not funny, I said.

There's nothing funny. He's here. I can see him.

You can see him.

I can.

Alright. What does he look like then?

Nice smile, clean face. He's blonde with two nice wrinkles on his forehead.

I felt my eyes widening as far as they could and my jaw started dropping.

He's wearing a white shirt and a grey jacket. Elegant, if you like.

Now there was a shockwave rising from the base of my spine up to my head. My face got all its warmth back, all at once, and my heart started its silly race again, and I strangled Mal's hand in mine. The description was right. That was Neil. Or it could have been. But it could have been almost everyone else, right? It was a game of chance.

Is that enough? Do you believe me now?

It's a nice description, I grumbled. But it could fit many people.

I can't hear him, but from what I get he's sorry that you felt ill? Fainted? At the funeral today?

My brain went into information overload. It was Neil. It was here. He was here. Next to me. All the time. I saw him. It wasn't fake. I saw him. I saw him. He saw me. He's here with me. I saw him and he's here. He's real. I don't believe it. He's here. He's not dead. He's dead. But he's here. But I can't see him. But *how*? *Why*?

I stopped to catch my breath and looked to my left where Neil was supposed to be, but saw nothing and extended my arm to touch the thin air and nothing happened and I squeezed Mal's hand even more and my knees were shaking again and I dragged Mal over to a bench and I was almost there when again my knees said We give up.

Lou? Louis? I heard Mal's voice from behind the curtains of my eyes. *Lou? Are you here?* Her voice was coming in, and I opened my eyes.

Twice in a day, I said.

Twice what?

I fainted at the funeral today. When I thought I saw – I paused, then blurted out, When I saw Neil.

You don't see him now though, do you?

I looked around. No, I don't see him, I said.

Okay.

Is he here?

Yes, he is.

Where?

Next to you, on the bench.

I looked at the empty bench. Hi, I said.

He's waving.

He is, isn't he.

Yes. How do you feel? Can you walk?

I think I can, I said, and stood up. I put my hand on Mal's shoulder, to keep myself upright.

She smiled and said Shall we?

How do you do it?

How do I do what? Walking? One foot after the other.

No. Seeing these things.

Oh. It runs in the family I suppose. Now walk with me.

We walked back to the hotel in silence until we got to her car. She clicked the key and the car beeped and she stood leaning against the door with her hands in her back pockets, looking at me. Tight black pants and sneakers, grey t-shirt, and a leather jacket. So beautiful. I wasn't sure what to say or whether to say anything, so she spoke,

So. You don't see him you say.

No. Not now.

But you did see him today.

I did, yes.

What changed?

Sorry?

What changed? Did you do something strange? Did you stand next to someone in particular?

No, I was alone. And no, nothing strange. But-

But?

Nothing.

Tell me.

Maybe it's nothing. I don't know.

You tell me and we'll decide together if it's nothing.

I drank tequila.

Tequila.

Yes.

But you drank tequila in my place as well. Did you see him there?

I, uh, I don't know. I felt him, I think.

You felt him. But you didn't tell.

I saw him.

You saw him.

I did.

She swung her head to the right and clenched her teeth so hard I heard the sound it made. She jumped away from the car and stood there and crossed her arms.

When I kissed you, she said.

When you kissed me, yes.

You saw him.

I did. He was behind you. God, oh my god. I saw him.

That's why you jumped away.

Yes. That's why.

She started laughing. She brought her hand to her forehead and closed her eyes.

What's funny? I said.

She stopped laughing and became all serious in a heartbeat. Hello? she said, I can see him?

You can see him. You can. It took me two seconds to realize what that meant. Oh, right! You can see him! So you knew!

I did.

You knew I saw him but you didn't say! Why didn't you say anything?

Because I thought you weren't seeing him or wanted to hide it from me. Which you did.

Yes but I did it because I didn't want you to think I was crazy! I said with a high-pitched voice.

Well, are you?

You tell me! So he was there the whole time! Wait, was he there the *whole* time?

I guess he was.

Neil, you sick fuck! I said. You're a bastard! Can you hear me? You're dead for fuck's sake! You don't sneak on your best friend! I started shouting at the air and waving my hands around.

I probably looked like the crazy one, and all of a sudden my perception of the crazy ones changed completely. Maybe they were just people that knew and saw more than me. I decided not to sit next to people talking to themselves on the buses anymore. I might step on their dead mother. My thoughts were interrupted by Mal, who said,

It's fine by me. He's laughing at you, by the way.

Well, it's not fine by me.

Leave him be, would you? He's dead anyway. Whatever keeps him *alive*, I guess.

Sorry. I'm not used to ghosts' behavior.

They're not either.

Oh.

So it was probably the tequila, huh?

I guess so. Wait, did you see him the first time we met? At the bar?

Yes.

Holy shit and you talked to me anyway?

Yes. She was playing with her hands, and had a grin on her face when she said I kinda talked to you because of him, actually.

You did? Why?

I felt you were *open*. Perceptive, if you want, about other places, other realities.

But I'm not.

Aren't you? If you can see him even when just drinking tequila it means something. It means you're receptive.

Receptive.

I don't know a better word. But that can play well.

I didn't reply.

So, do you wanna try?

Try what?

To communicate with him?

Like a seance?

More like we buy tequila and get shitfaced at my house.

Is that a thing? I mean, a thing in occult circles or whatever?

A thing?

Like a seance.

I wouldn't know. I kinda work alone. But you function when under the effect of tequila apparently. Make peace with it.

I'm a drunk medium.

You can call yourself whatever you want. Let's go, she said, opening the door of her car.

I pointed at my car and walked towards it and took the duffel bag with my things in it and then sat in her car. She drove left and right and straight and left and stopped at a drive-through to get tequila and I was quiet and kept looking around and at the rearview mirror. Once Neil and I were on a road trip. On the way back from whatever place we went, he was hammered and slept in the backseat for a while. I stopped to pick up a hitchhiker, a young man with a face that didn't look like one belonging to a serial killer. The man jumped in the front seat. We started talking and I kept looking at the rearview mirror to check when Neil would wake up. The young man noticed it and asked me, Why are you checking the mirror? But he didn't have the time to hear the answer back – Neil woke up and jumped onto him. I swear I felt the thump of the man's heart, almost smashing his chest. I burst out in laughter. The guy swiftly punched Neil in the face, then opened the door while the car was moving. And jumped out. I looked at Neil in disbelief and we stopped, but the guy ran far away because when you are hitchhiking you're either the good guy or the killer, and we probably gave the wrong impression. Since then, I would check my car's back seat every time I went on a road trip with Neil – to see if he was there. And now, that was what I was doing. Looking back, hoping to catch a glimpse of Neil.

I can see my dead friend, I thought. Not all the time, but I can. I haven't lost him. I'm not crazy. I'm not crazy.

He's there in the back if you're wondering, Mal said.

I checked the rearview mirror again – on the lookout. Nothing. Can they ride in cars? I asked.

So it seems.

So we're going to get drunk?

You are. That's the plan.

And then?

And then you'll probably talk to him.

Can't you?

Apparently not. Her eyes squinted and she closed her lips together tightly. She wasn't happy about it.

Did you ever? Talk to ghosts, I mean.

I try to do it, sometimes.

You do. Of course you do. How does it work?

You talk to them.

And how come you can't talk to Neil?

I can talk to him, he just doesn't reply.

And why's that?

I don't know. I don't make the rules.

Alright.

We finally arrived at her place. I took the duffel bag with me and we went inside. The piece of paper with my number was exactly where I'd left it.

Apparently, destiny wasn't through with me and Mal. Apparently, I had more story with her. Maybe some people are destined to come into your life and there's no need for you to act, but I promised myself to always take the phone numbers of people I connected with. If she hadn't called me, I would have probably forgotten about her. Eventually, we forget everything, until we forget ourselves.

Now I was in her living room and she disappeared into the bathroom and said, I'll be back in a second. I sat on the couch and looked around, but didn't see Neil. I saw the pile of books, so I got up and walked over to look at the titles. I recognized some of them: The Bible; The Qur'an; The Book of the Dead; Dianetics; The Book of Mormon. I didn't recognize some of the others with strange words in unknown languages and unpronounceable names like Popol Vuh,

Pyrgi Tablets, Kojiki. It wouldn't take a genius to realize that they were all religious books. Or books about the occult. Or books about what's not here but *there*. Mallory was definitely informed about those things. I was trying to figure out the name of another book when she came out of the bathroom with only a big white towel around her body and said, If your friend tries to get into the shower with me again I won't help him.

What? Neil! I shouted.

I'm joking, she said laughing. He didn't.

Oh.

You should relax a bit, you know, she said with a dry voice.

How can I relax? I said, reacting to her wit. You might know your stuff—I said, pointing at the books—but I don't.

Yes, I know my stuff and that's exactly why you should relax.

Alright. Help him you said?

Yes.

Help him do what?

Leave this world.

For?

For the next? For oblivion? For whatever's there, I don't know.

Can you really do it?

We'll see. How did he die?

Heart attack.

Heart attack. So young. What happened?

I was there.

You were.

I was. I found him in my bathtub, dead.

What was he doing in your bathtub?

I don't know. I found him there.

Do you normally find your friends dead in your bathtub?

No.

So how did he end up there?

She said this and then looked at the window. Then she squinted her eyes and I thought she wasn't looking at the window but at Neil, or whatever was left of him, so I asked,

Is he there?

Can't you guess? I think he's trying to talk. I can't hear you! she shouted.

What?

Maybe he wants to talk about his death. Get the bottle, she said, looking at the tequila, and disappeared into the bedroom.

I opened the bottle and went to the kitchen to grab two glasses and poured. She was back with jeans and a sweater on and she tied her hair up and came close. She looked at the glasses and took a shot of hers. I did the same, and poured two more, while saying,

Wasn't I supposed to get drunk all by myself?

I'll stop here. You go on.

Wait, I can't drink the whole bottle. Not alone.

I won't drink more. You will.

Alright, I replied.

My life and actions were not mine, not anymore; were they ever mine, I wondered. I took another glass. Then another. Then a third, or was it the fourth already? I hadn't eaten since the morning. Fifth glass. Still no sign of my ghostly friend. I poured the next glass and said,

I do't see no hear a'thin. T'isn't working.

It's getting you drunk, she replied. Don't you see him?

I do not, I said, and miscalculated the force of my hand and smashed the glass down on the table. I cut my right hand and blood poured from it and the pain kicked me out of my drunkenness and Mal moved quickly out of the chair to the kitchen to get a towel for my hand and I turned to go to the bathroom and

Neil was standing there. Right there.

And no, I didn't faint this time. I was drunk and lucid at the same time. I didn't scream, didn't run. I stared at him. I could see him. He looked *normal*. Alive. Nothing like you'd expect a ghost to look like. No fuzzy borders, no transparency, just real.

You're here, I said, simply.

I am, he replied.

I heard a voice from the kitchen saying What! and it was Mal and she said I heard him! and Oh my god you can see him!

Yes. Yes, I can see him, I said.

Louis, Neil said.

Yes.

Do you remember what happened?

I was silent.

You puked all over me, buddy. That's not fair.

It was a snort at first. Then a sound like blowing raspberries, then a fat, hard laugh, while my hands grabbed my belly and my eyes filled up with tears of joy. Neil was here, and not just here but also cracking jokes.

I did, didn't I? I replied, still laughing.

Yes. But you cried as well.

I did that too.

Thank you. For being there.

Mal sat, studying my face, with her legs crossed under her on the couch, and then she reached for a glass of tequila and kept all her thoughts to herself, a silent spectator of the otherworldly show.

Do you remember what happened, Lou? Neil asked.

Apart from the morning after?

Yes.

It's cloudy.

We were drunk.

Indeed.

We went up to your neighbor's.

We did.

And I went in first, Neil said, and there it was—standing still, black against the black—and then it looked at me and it had no eyes and I felt it entering deep into me and I felt like someone's hand was squeezing me inside, cracking my heart open.

I was now as silent as Mal. Neil continued,

And then I'm there and you're there but you don't see me. I talk but you don't hear me. Then I see myself on the ground and I realize. And I scream and scream and scream, but only silence comes out of my throat, and finally you see me, but then you pass out.

I tend to do that a lot lately, I said.

I noticed. I've been with you ever since, but you only saw me again here. In this room. Do you remember?

I remember, and I thought I was crazy, I replied.

You weren't. Did you see it?

It? I saw the neighbor. And a huge crow.

Oh. I only saw the crow.

No, the neighbor was there.

Mallory interrupted us. Hey? I'm still here. Would you care to tell me what's happening?

We're recalling the night he died, I said. We saw some strange things that scared us. More Neil really, I said, pointing at him.

What kind of things? Mal asked.

A giant crow and my neighbor dressed up as – I reached for my mouth, a reflex, then said, This is crazy, okay? As you would imagine Death, the Grim Reaper.

Mallory spit out the tequila she was drinking and her eyes widened and she jumped off the couch and went to the counter and took the bottle and drank directly from it, and her eyes were open wide but there was no fear in them, just curiosity.

He what?, she shouted.

I recalled the night for her, trying to keep all the details square. The smell, the unnatural darkness, the big, tall bird, and Skinny Guy—dressed up as Death itself. The darkness and dust and his bony hands and the blade. Mal and I passed the bottle back and forth and I was fighting my own mind to believe what I was looking at—at what I'd seen.

And what I was about to see, maybe.

You met Death, Mal said.

I don't know. He was sure dressed up like it.

You probably did. You wouldn't be the first one. Her eyes sparkled.

Not the first one?

To meet whatever it is that you wanna call it. Before their time runs out. There are all sorts of tales; haven't you heard any?

I heard some. How do you know I wasn't just hallucinating? I asked her.

Because you're here talking to a ghost, so that's enough for me to believe you.

I see.

What else? Did you talk to him? I knew you were the right guy!

Thanks. For the right guy thing. I didn't really manage to talk to him, but I definitely said something.

Were you scared?

Uh, yeah. I was. But I was also drunk.

And you saw something else. A giant bird, you say?

I know it sounds crazy.

Lou, again with that. We're in my living room talking to a ghost. Nothing can be crazier. This changes it. Hell, this changes everything! I never came across such a, a, - such a thing!

She started moving around the room in excitement. I looked at Neil and wanted to hug him, but the rules of these things apparently deny it and you can't touch a ghost and he can't touch you, but you can look into each other's eyes and that's more than every other human being I know can say. I started laughing again, and said,

And the funny, or scary, thing is I believe he was living upstairs.

What? What did you say? Mal broke out of her train of thought and sat back down on the couch, looking at me.

That he was living upstairs. Death.

Death. Upstairs. But you stumbled across him because you wanted to go into your neighbor's apartment, right?

No, well yes. He was the neighbor.

What?

He was the neighbor. You see, I'd seen him a couple of times and he was this skinny guy and he looked very weird and Neil never saw him but only imagined him from what I told him. So that night me and Neil were drunk and thought he was a devil's worshipper or something so we went upstairs but we didn't think-

She interrupted me, and said You saw it—Death—more than once. Her face was long and pale and filled with disbelief.

He was living upstairs, I told you.

But you're now telling me that he was like me and you, that he was a normal guy.

I wouldn't say normal, would I, Neil?

My friend shook his head. Mal stood up straight and shouted, Yes, but that's it! You saw Death, you bumped into him more than once, and he was normal to you? Her hands were wavering between her face and mine.

I, yes, he was normal, a bit weird.

We have to find him.

Her voice suddenly was flat and monotone, like she was just reading the morning news. An emptiness of feeling, a lack of empathy – whatever it was, it made me shiver down my spine. For as much as I was drunk in that moment, Mal's words brought me back to lucidity in a heartbeat. I figured I still had alcohol in my blood as Neil was there—silent—and I looked at Mal, but couldn't find any words that would have made for a good reply. Finally, Neil said,

Are you crazy, lady?

Mal didn't reply.

Is she crazy? Neil said to me.

Mal spoke and said, I say we perform a ritual. To summon it.

We summon it. Death, Neil replied.

It's all in the books, you see? Mal said. Everyone reaches out to gods with prayers and rituals. And some people, sometimes they get an answer. I say we reach out to Death. She paused then added To help your friend pass over, right?

And then what? We say hello? Neil said.

Neil's right, I replied. What then?

Mal brought her hands to her face and let her body fall back on the couch. I never did the ritual that way, but it might be just what's needed.

You did stuff like this before? I asked.

It was different. You trust me, don't you?

I think I do.

And I did. For strange chemicals flood the brain after we mate with someone – a beginning of hormones and survival instinct, so powerful and ancient that we misread it as love. And having a heart that is just waiting to be touched helps. I did trust her, even if she was a total stranger, even though her beautiful eyes were sometimes distant, as though her thoughts were in an oblivious world where no one can set foot.

Is it going to be dangerous? I said.

Maybe, but we'll survive. That's what counts, right?

Right.

We all stood there, silent, everyone contemplating what Mal had said. Everything we look for, everything we do, is all a play to keep death at bay, but this lady here was ready to face it. Neil said,

Alright. If that's what's needed for me to go, let's call that thing.

And I took a long, long drink from the bottle.

six

The dusk and the drinks pushed me to sleep while I was still on the couch. When I woke up it was the middle of the night and the cold chilled my bones. Mal's bedroom door was open. I looked around and whispered *Neil?* but there was no reply from the darkness. I stood up and walked to Mal's room. From the door I could see her body under the blankets, moving rhythmically up and down and up and down, and if I listened very carefully I could hear her breathing. I sat on the bed and moved the blanket and slipped under it.

I didn't touch her.

I lay there, looking at the ceiling. My eyes didn't want to close and my mind didn't want to surrender to the oblivion of sleep. I laid there until I reached those fading hours in which all thoughts and all feelings and all suffering darkly find their place.

And then my body surrendered and I slept next to her again.

When I opened my eyes she was no longer there. I heard noises and smelled coffee so I got up, pulled on my pants, and went into the living room. Mal was sitting on the floor, surrounded by opened books, frantically moving from one page to another and from one book to another. In her hand was a notebook—the same one I used to leave the note. She was scribbling furiously page after page, so caught in her moment that she didn't even notice me walking behind her to the kitchen to pour myself some coffee. I leaned on the counter with the cup in my hands. I waited a couple of minutes, scanning the room, trying to figure out if I could still see Neil, if he was still there. Nothing in the air but molecules of dust dancing in the rays of light, unaware. Like Mal. Finally, I gave up and started talking,

Good morning.

Oh. Hi. Didn't see you there, she replied.

I noticed.

Yes. Sorry. Her hands kept scribbling and her eyes reading.

No problem. Is Neil around?

She glanced superficially around and said He's not here.

Her voice was flat and dry. She was in her world and I was just outside. No means of real communication. Two books close to each other that can't possibly know what the other is about.

So, we have a ritual here to plan, I said.

That's what I am doing.

Then what?

What do you mean?

I mean, why.

To help your friend, she said, without looking up from the books.

Help him. How?

She dropped her notebook. Her arms joined together, knotting each other, and finally she looked at me – two marbles of blue fire. She said,

You don't know, do you? *That's* why I am doing this. Because *I* do. *I* know. So let me do this.

I scoffed but said, Sorry. Didn't mean to upset you. And while I was saying this, I moved further away, physically.

Her brow wrinkled. I'm not upset, she replied.

You seem like it. Maybe we should call this off.

You don't know what you're talking about.

I don't. That's true.

I've done this for a long time.

Contacting dead people? I said.

Sort of. Moving spirits around.

I see, I replied, and my eyes took refuge in the cup not to face hers.

She didn't speak.

So, how do you move spirits around? I said.

Humanity has tried to contact the other world since the beginning of history. Some people see it, some people try not to. Others stumble upon it, like you.

Like me.

And now you know. Now you've seen. There's not just your body, the material world around you. There's something more.

That's a comforting thought, actually.

Hold your horses. It ain't that pretty.

What? I said.

Now that we were talking about these things, the things she apparently liked to do, her expression relaxed a bit. She replied,

To be dead. To be a spirit with no body, with no direction.

Like in the movies. You haunt things. Places.

You know why?

Why?

She got up and came next to me. Gently and with care she took the cup from my hands and put it on the counter. She looked at me, straight, and said,

Because it's scary. Because it's lonely. Because no one sees you and no one remembers you and after a while you start doubting you ever *really* existed. So you find a person or a place or an object, and you attach yourself to it with all your energy. But after a while, the place, the object, it becomes the only thing you know.

What do you mean? I said.

I mean you forget who you were. What you were. And you don't know anything else, you lose yourself. And there's no coming back, no going forward.

I looked at her eyes, blue and deep and cold and beautiful. Silent ponds of her soul.

So we want to help your friend here to stay not. To cling not. To let go.

Where? I said.

Wherever.

Is there a paradise? A hell?

Whatever is there.

Do you believe?

In a god?

Yes.

I guess, she replied.

But in all your studies, have you ever-

No.

I repeated her word. No.

Do *you* believe? she asked.

I never stopped long enough to form an opinion. I guess we'll find out eventually.

We will.

She smiled at me like you'd smile at a kid after a lecture, when he finally understood he'd done something wrong, and then she went back to her books. I went back to my cup, which was almost as cold as the thought of forgetting who you are, what you are. I poured the coffee down the sink and walked through the room to the bedroom. My bag was there. I opened it and there were no clean clothes for me that day. Without thinking, I opened the first drawer to look for a t-shirt. I found only female underwear. I opened the second drawer and then I realized what I was doing - even if I found a t-shirt, it wouldn't fit. She came in the room and I didn't notice it until she said with firm voice,

What are you doing?
Hey. I was looking for a t-shirt.
In my drawers? she frowned.
I know, it's stupid. I must still be slow from last night.
Didn't you ever learn to respect other people's privacy?
I said I was sorry.

She walked quickly to the dresser and opened the first drawer. She moved the underwear around and took out a small jewelry box. She looked inside and closed it again and kept it with her. She closed the drawer with a quick movement that created a small *thud!.* Shivers of discomfort rippled on my back, caused by her behavior. She went back into the other room without saying a word, but keeping the box close to her chest. I'm not a thief! I shouted, and laughed uncomfortably. I still felt pretty shaken from everything that had happened until that point. Trying to justify the icy wall that I felt already growing between me and Mal, I found excuses. Maybe I was misreading her reactions, or maybe she was too focused on what she was doing. After all, I was the stranger in her house and she was trying to help me. After all, I was the one seeing ghosts and death.

I went back to my bag and took out the shirt I wore at Neil's funeral. I sniffed it. It wasn't fresh, but it wasn't awful either. I went to the bathroom and took a long, warm shower. When I was out of the water I felt better. I got dressed and looked in the mirror. The shirt was all creases and folds, and the pants were dirty at the ends. I did not like the man I saw in the mirror. Neil would always wear a blazer and a freshly ironed shirt. I always said he was too formal. I always told him to relax his style a bit. But he would always smile back at my remarks, pretending to tie up an invisible tie.

This was who he was. This was the image he projected and the image I'll remember. The image – absurdly – that he still has after life.

Right there, with me looking back at myself from the mirror, I promised to always be dressed as I'd like to be remembered.

Because you never know when you're going to meet the end.

The ritual had to take place in my apartment. Mal, who was clearly in charge, said something about energy and the last place where Neil was alive and such. Reluctantly, Mal agreed to go back to the city in my car. During the whole trip I kept glancing at the rearview mirror trying to see Neil, who wasn't with us anymore. We drove a few miles without talking, without looking at each other, just looking at the road and at the other vehicles and the landscape and whatever was outside of the car. I had thoughts running around in my head, and thought Mal could help make some order of them, so I said,

I was thinking.

About?

About the crow.

The one you saw when Neil died.

Yes.

What about it?

If I saw what I saw, this one was a giant black bird.

How giant?

Like a football player.

And he spoke to you.

And to Neil, I said, looking at nothing in the rearview mirror.

That's okay.

How is a giant bird okay?

I mean. It's expected.

Would you expect a giant crow?

No. I don't know. It's like black cats and owls. Crows. It's said that they can go from here to there or see things we can't. They're psychopomps.

Psychic Pomps?

Psychopomps. It's Greek. It means guide of the soul.

Oh.

Every culture has one.

So where do they guide the souls to?

Wherever there's a place for them, I guess.

I kept driving in silence.

The Greeks had Thanatos, who was a beautiful young boy. He'd pass the souls to Charon, who would collect them on his boat and cross the unearthly river Styx. The Egyptians had Anubis, half human, half dog. He'd go the extra mile and weigh your soul against a feather, to see if you were a worthy one.

I doubt many people passed the test.

But psychopomps don't judge, they merely act as a connection. They're the first way humans had to figure out death, and that's why they're usually an embodiment of nature. That's why Anubis is half human. Only humans judge.

Do all these things actually exist? I asked.

I don't know. You know that the crow exists. And that death has an anthropomorphic embodiment. I believe that's enough.

Does the crow belong to one particular tradition?

Comes from Europe, I'd say. They had this goddess of war and death and fertility: the Morrighan.

What about her?

Well, she used to fly over battlefields in the form of a giant bird. A crow.

And?

And she'd try to seduce the most powerful warriors and sway battles one way or another.

Seems dangerous, I said.

She is in the tales. But tales are made by humans, for humans. She was also a goddess of sovereignty, of fertility, of good luck.

So, the crow was the Morrighan, I said.

Maybe. They also say that the Morrighan was a trio of deities, which might explain the difference in meanings. I believe the crow was just the designated psychopomp for that night. Neil's own death, if you wish.

Right. Well, it did a shitty job, I said, trying to catch Neil in the rearview mirror with no luck.

I'm more fascinated by the other one. Death as we know it. It wore a robe, right? she asked.

The night that everything happened he did.

But you saw him in normal clothes.

I did.

Black clothes.

Full black.

Okay, she said. She got rid of her shoes and put her feet up on the windshield. Do you know about the Black Plague? she asked.

Uh, not much.

It was a long time ago. It's when the first depictions of Death as a skeleton with a black mantle started to show up. It also had an hourglass, to remind you of the passing of time, and a scythe. It comes from the farmer culture of Europe at that time. The Black Plague killed twenty-five million people.

That's a lot of people.

Especially back then. It was terrible. People would catch it and they'd start to rot before dying. Your flesh would rot and leave only your bones.

So that's why he's a skeleton.

Probably.

Well, from what I've seen they got him almost right.

Almost. So you had no clue about all this?

No. But I figured Death would look like that.

How come?

I don't know really. It's a memory from childhood. My dad.

She kept looking at me without saying anything.

He loved this band; I don't remember their name. On the album he played over and over there was a picture of a skeleton dressed up like the guy I've seen. Robe, scythe, the works. When I was a kid I was scared of that picture. Even if the song that played said I shouldn't be.

So now you know where they got the representation of Death.

I looked at her. How do you know all these things?

It's a long story. You don't wanna hear it.

I want to; I have time.

It's a family thing, she said, trying to dismiss the subject. Her hands were playing with a small, golden necklace she was wearing.

Are all the people in your family like you?

They were.

Oh. I'm sorry.

Don't be, she said.

So you're alone.

I am. Well, I have a twin sister.

A twin sister? Really? Is she like you?

She can be.

What's her name?

Angelene.

I guess you're not close.

You're right, she said, and slid down in her seat, moving it backwards. Do you mind if I sleep? I didn't get much last night, she said.

No problem, I replied, and kept driving.

I parked the car after almost four hours of driving and the sudden lack of motion woke Mal. Being back in my apartment gave me a strange feeling. The bathroom door was ajar and I did everything I could for the first ten minutes to avoid going in there. When I finally did everything was normal. It was a bathroom. No bodies, no blood, nothing. Mal got her books out on the table, and I started brewing some coffee. Do we have tequila? she asked. We didn't. So out I went to buy not one but two bottles of tequila. When I got back, Mallory was scribbling in her notebook again and didn't even look up. I made the two bottles clink and she smiled and went back with her face in the books and her hands on the notebook. She was quiet; the only noise you could hear was her writing. I sat on the chair for a moment. Looked around. I had no part in this; I felt left out. I took one of Mal's books, opened it to a random page. I read the words.

The golden crow lights on the western huts
Evening drums beat out the shortness of life
There are no inns on the road to the grave -
Whose is the house I go to tonight?

I stood there with the book open, reading and rereading those four lines. Where were we going tonight? Mal noticed the book in my hand and spoke to me,

It's very ancient, you know.

The book?

Yes. Not this one of course. The original.

Oh. I see.

It's from the far east. Japan. They have a different perception of things. For them the ritual is the most important thing.

I listened.

You see, in Japanese culture, everything is ritualized. They celebrate the *seppuku*, the honorable death that you can inflict on yourself. They realize that just existing is not possible; it must be done in a certain way. The ritual is all.

Whenever Mal talked about rituals and ancient cultures she was a different person. Her face would get harder, thornier, but her voice would be calmer. She spoke slowly, with lots of pauses, trying to emphasize the knowledge she had—the power of rituals, the power of history, the power of the unseen. But I could see that behind her blue eyes she was as scared as me. It doesn't matter the amount of knowledge, for the more you know the less you understand. My mind rushed with those thoughts while I listened to her, and I asked,

Is that important to us?

It is. What we're doing is trying to find a ritual. Something that will bind death to our will.

Is that even possible?

Maybe. People have tried to subjugate otherworldly beings for centuries. Even Time itself.

What if it works?

I hope it does.

Then what do we do?

I think you should drink.

What?

Tequila. Drink.

I'm fed up with alcohol, Mal.

Can you see your friend?

No, I replied, and sighed.

Then drink.

I went to the kitchen and opened the bottle. I took out two glasses, but Mal shook her head. I poured the tequila just for me, golden and cold and I drank it down in one shot. Poured another one. Drank it. I repeated it three times more and like magic I started seeing Neil's edges appear from thin air and finally he was standing clear before me. I smiled at him. Then I looked at Mal again, and said,

I'm sorry about your sister.

What?

I said, I'm sorry if I brought up your sister and you hate her. Or don't talk to her, or whatever it is.

Mal closed the notebook and said, She left me. She left me and my mom after Dad died. To go to Las Vegas. To be a stripper—Mal's face twisted with disgust. She continued, and the pace of her words quickened to cover her distress—Mom got sick. And my sister didn't care! She came back only towards the end. I begged her to stay, to help me. But she left again. I haven't spoken with her since. Mal's face was red and she probably felt it as she raised her hands to her cheeks, as though to check the temperature of her burning skin.

I muttered some words without meaning, and managed to finish with, I'm sorry.

Don't be for me. Be for her. Mal's voice was calmer.

Was it a long time ago?

I don't really want to talk about it, okay?

Sorry, I said, and then tried to change the subject. So, are we doing a ritual?

Yes.

A seance?

Seances are bullshit.

How do you know?

Have you ever done one?

Yes. I was a kid. With a ouija board.

Did it work?

No. We were making things up to scare the other kids.

Well then.

I thought if you're, *gifted*, then it might work.

Well, you can see Neil, right? You're gifted. And it didn't work.

So what's the plan? I said with a touch of impatience. I wanted this thing to be quick and painless.

I'm working on it, she said. You go talk to Neil. Keep him aware of the surroundings. Of what's happening. Of who he is. Do you have a lucky charm?

What do you mean?

A lucky charm. An object you like that has meaning to you.

No.

It can be anything. You can bind Neil's spirit to it. To keep him around.

Why would I do that?

Just in case, you know.

In case what?

In case this thing doesn't work and you want to hold on to your friend for just a little longer, she said, looking at me.

She went back to her books, opened her notebook, and started writing again. I poured another glass of tequila and noticed that the bottle was half empty already. I went towards the window and Neil followed. He cast no shadow. That was the only thing that, to my eyes, was different than having him there for real. He was there for me, the whole time. He was there for the deaths of my parents. *After the first death, there is no more*, but it's not true. There are more and more and more; the first is only the beginning. Everything has an expiration date. Everything is impermanent.

I swallowed the rest of the tequila in the glass and started kissing the bottle directly.

It was late afternoon before Mallory emerged from her books. I managed to keep my alcohol intoxication stable and steady, just tipsy enough to keep talking with Neil. The words wouldn't have shown he was dead. Our talks were the same. I pushed the topic of what we were about to do as far as possible, but now it was time. Mal told us to get prepared. I took two more sips of tequila, my best preparation. Neil stood at the window, looking out at a world he wasn't part of anymore. Mal disappeared into the bedroom for ten minutes, then came out dressed completely in black. Tight pants and sweater and trainers. Her bag was next to the door, closed, neat. She gave me a list of objects she needed to find. Dark curtains. Mirrors. We moved the mirror from the bathroom, the one from the bedroom. Brought them into the living room, close to each other. I went out of my apartment and into the hallway. There was a huge mirror there. Without being seen I slid the mirror in through my door. I had no black curtains. She told me a blanket would do. I gathered up all my bedspreads and took them into the living room. We started hanging them, blocking the light coming from the window. Blocking all the light. It had to be done thoroughly – Mal would question every small hole of light coming in. After a couple of hours the sun was completely set and the room was so dark you could barely see. She looked around satisfied, and said,

That's good.

Good for what? I replied, I can't see a thing.

That's how a room's supposed to look when you want to call upon the dead.

Oh.

The darkness and the mirrors. Let your eyes adjust. Ancient Americans used smaller rooms, but the principle is the same. This serves to induce trance. To communicate with things you can't normally see or hear.

So are we ready?

Mal nodded. Neil nodded.

Louis, you might want to play your part here, she said.

What do I have to do?

You have to stall it.

Stall what?

Death.

I laughed, genuinely, and then said Great. How?

It might come with its henchman. It might come alone.

Alright. So, what do I do?

You saw it and you're alive. It might want to finish the job.

What? Now you're scaring me.

Trust me. Everything will be fine.

Huh. Well, so what do I do again?

You stall it. I need time. If we're lucky the room will help me communicate with it. And then we can help Neil.

How do I stall it?

I don't know. Talk to it. Ask questions. Why are we here? Is there a God? The usual stuff.

Okay. Why are we here? Where are we going? Basically you want me to give the Grim Reaper stoner talks.

Mal didn't reply.

What now? I asked.

She kneeled. Sit on the chair, she said. I sat on the chair. She gave me a glass of water. Drink it, she said. I drank it. She opened the zipper on her bag. Took out a black cloth, rolled it. Unrolled it. There was a knife. What are you doing? I said. It's necessary, she replied, and held the handle of the knife in her right hand and closed her left hand on the blade. She quickly moved the blade out of her grasp and blood started flowing onto the black cloth that she'd carefully placed on the floor. She kept her left hand closed. She cleaned one side of the blade. The other one was still red with blood. She took her cell phone. Opened it. I was sitting still and I felt Neil behind me. We didn't dare move, scared of ruining the ritual. My head started spinning and I thought I'd had too much tequila. A voice on the other end of the phone answered. Mal started talking. She gave my house address to the phone. Then she said Someone's been stabbed, and ended the call.

I looked at her. She looked back. Deep blue eyes, cold lakes. I wanted to ask if the cut on her hand was that bad or if she wanted to call this off, but I didn't have time as she took a deep breath and came closer and said I'm sorry, and stabbed me.

seven

I didn't feel any pain. Not in that moment. Not in my body. Her eyes were still on me and the knife was still in me and I wrapped my hands around hers. Why? I asked. She pulled the knife out and put the blade in her left hand and my blood was in her blood. I instinctively covered the wound in my gut with both my hands. A dark spot was enlarging by the second and I felt the warmth of my blood flowing onto my legs. Mal cleaned the knife on the black cloth and rolled it up again and put it in the bag. Neil's face became enraged, and then he wasn't Neil anymore but a black shadow whirling around Mal, who didn't seem to be bothered by it at all. Why? I asked again, and tried to stand up. Mal put her hand on my shoulder and kept me on the chair. I was losing energy fast and my eyes were feeling heavier by the second. Then the pain arrived. It was a punch at first, and a thousand punches immediately afterwards. With every blow came a needle deep inside, and every needle would rhythmically explode in a firework of pain.

Why? I shouted.

There's no time, Louis. It's part of the plan. I called 911 in time. You'll be fine.

Her face was calm. The only words out of my mouth were Why me?

You see ghosts and otherworldly beings. And you're still alive. Chances are you're a perfect fit.

I trusted you.

And you did well. You'll see. You'll survive. I need you to. Don't move.

She said those last words and sat down, waiting. I could feel my blood slipping out and my mind started drifting apart and I wanted to stand up and run and beat her up for what she'd done. I was cold. Very cold.

The room got darker and colder and covered with a thin mist. Mal was sitting still, frozen in position. Neil was a blur above Mal. He was also still. The pain decreased to a more bearable burden. I moved my hands away from my belly, and that's when I saw him.

The Grim Reaper. Standing right in front of me, in his high uniform. Before I could speak, he opened his mouth, and said,

Nice room you have prepared here.

Ehr. Uh. Cough - Those were my first words to Death. His voice was the same: an indefinable age, or, better, all ages together.

Are you afraid? he said.

I am. I am.

Do not be. It will probably be over soon.

I don't want it to be over.

No one wants that, my boy. He moved closer. His blade was glowing, even with no light source around.

She stabbed me, I said, pointing at Mal.

She is a keeper then, he said, with a snort of laughter.

Great, he's a wise guy, I thought. We wanted to call for you, I said, and coughed again - there was blood in my mouth.

I always come; there is not the need to call.

Do you come for everyone?

Everyone has his own death. And he must die that death alone. Alas, the desire to have a death of one's own is becoming a rare occurrence. Shortly, it will be as rare as a life of one's own. He paused and then added, I did not say that; someone of yours did.

So that's it? That's my time? I said.

We will see. She called an ambulance, did she?

She said she did.

Good girl.

She stabbed me.

You wanted to see me, you said?

I did.

Why so abruptly then?

I wanted you to help Neil.

Oh yes. He died the other day.

Yes, sir.

That is how life is supposed to go, my boy.

So you can't do anything?

What do you expect me to do? He is dead, is he not?

But he's still here!

Eventually he will not be.

What can I do?

What do you want to do?

I want to live.

That is to be decided, my boy. He took a chair and sat in front of me.

What were you doing in that apartment? I said.

What was I doing? Very funny. What are *you* doing in an apartment?

I live in one. I guess.

You do not know if you live in an apartment or not? Are we not in your apartment? he asked, pointing a bony finger around.

We are.

Well then.

I mean, what's Death doing living in an apartment?

I was not living *there*. *There* is only where you saw me.

I saw you more than once, I said.

You did indeed.

How is that possible?

I am more intrigued by the fact that you do not see me more often.

But why me?

Why me, why me, why me? That is your favorite question. He rolled up the sleeves of the robe, revealing his skeletal hands. Well, why not? Why would it be that things cannot happen to you? he said. His voice was calm, monotone.

Am I going to die?

Why, are you in a hurry?

No.

Then relax and enjoy.

Enjoy?

Do whatever makes you comfortable. He waved his hands around, pointing at nothing in particular.

I looked around the room. Mal and Neil, frozen in a still frame. Can they see you? I said.

Who? The ghost and the lady? No, they cannot.

Why?

They are not dying. Or are already dead. Or do not want to. Your pick.

Can you make them see you?

I cannot make anyone do anything. They can see me if they want though.

What are we doing?

We are waiting to see if you will survive or not. I bet not.

That's not comforting.

Well, I am here.

I remembered Mal's words. Stall him. Could I trust her? She did call an ambulance. Maybe it was part of the plan. I was trying to think of something. But Death spoke,

Do you like games?

Do I like games?

Are you deaf? Yes, do you like to play games?

I suppose I do, I replied.

Good. We shall play.

Play?

Hello?, he said, while knocking with his bony hands on my head, then continued, Yes, play. Is there any game you like most?

I don't know.

What about chess?

A chess game?

A bit cliché, is it? But oh, I love that game. He put his hands into his robe and pulled out a small chessboard with magnetic pieces. A travel chessboard. He started aligning the pieces with his thin hands, and when everything was set up, he adjusted the chessboard on his lap and turned it with the white pieces towards me.

I am black, he said.

Wait, are we playing now? I asked.

Why, do you have anything better to do?

No, but I mean. I'm not a great player.

Oh, but you can play a game, can you? I hope you can. I get so bored.

I can play chess, yes.

Very good! He let go of the scythe and rested it on the ground, between he and Mal, who seemed to be in a slightly different pose, like she was slowly moving. What now? he said.

Nothing. It's like she's moving, I said, looking at her.

She probably is.

What?

We're just in a fold of time. For you it has almost stopped. The rest of the world is spinning. Your move.

Isn't there supposed to be a wager? I said.

A wager. If you find it more amusing, why not? The usual?

The usual?

All that you humans want is to live.

Oh. *That* usual.

Yes.

What would it be? Just to spell it out, you know.

If I win, you die. If you win, you survive. That simple, he said.

I looked at the chess pieces. Then at Mal. Then at the blur above her that was Neil. I was doing all this for a reason. I looked at Death. Wait, I said.

What?

Let's double the bet.

And how can you possibly double it?

If I win, I survive. And my friend does too.

Death looked at me. His eyes were black and still. And if I win? he said.

If you win, you take me. And Neil. And Mallory there.

He turned for a moment to look at Mallory. Then he looked at me. Then at the chessboard. Then at me again. He crossed his arms and brought a hand to his chin. He got rid of the hood and showed his face. Skinny Guy. You never know. He paused then said,

Your friend is not really in the game anymore, is he? And it would not be really polite to get the girl *now*. However - and he turned the pieces again, white to his side, while saying this - I *always* win. That is how it goes. Sorry about the spoiler. But to stir things up, I accept your bet, if that gives you more motivation. He moved a pawn.

Game on, I said. *Stall him,* I thought. I paused for what seemed an eternity, then moved my pawn.

I know you have all the time, my boy. But do not make this boring, all right?

I won't.

He looked at the chessboard, pondering his next move. I kept my eyes on the chessboard, but my eyes caught Mal. She was now moving more quickly. Moving towards us. Death placed his hand on another pawn, and left it there. Then he raised it and began to move it.

In that exact moment I saw Mal moving faster and faster and when she got so close that I saw her figure overlapping the Reaper's shape a *bang* filled my ears like someone had fired a gun right next to my head. The air that had been frozen became normal again and the first thing I noticed was the terrible, unbearable pain from the wound and I saw Mal looking straight at me. Death seemed caught by surprise by Mal's action, and let the pawn fall on a square and it seemed to me that he was disappearing. Mal didn't seem to notice that Death was here. Her face was pale but her cheeks were red and her body was shaking and sweaty. She looked at the knife in her hand and tightened her grip. She looked at me, and said, trembling,

I felt something different. It might just have worked this time.

I tried to reply, but all I managed to get out of my mouth was a gurgle.

I have to go, but I'll see you again, won't I? and kissed me on the cheek.

On the ground I could still see the chessboard. All the pieces remained in position, thanks to the magnetic board. I couldn't see much anymore, but I heard Mal stepping out of the apartment and a faint wail that I hoped belonged to a siren approaching to save me and with my last strength I moved enough to let my body slide to the ground. Death's piece was down; his move was made. My turn. I moved my queen all the way.

Checkmate.

I'm lying on a wooden table. I can't move. It's dark all around and I'm cold. I can feel the wood under my whole skin and that makes me I realize I'm naked. My eyes adjust to the dark and I see the puff of my breath in the air.

I feel steps behind me and I try to turn my head but I can't. There's a foul smell of alcohol and sweat that makes me scared and I shiver. I can see a black, tall figure coming closer and closer. It approaches quickly and circles me three times and all I can see is the white of its eyes and the white of its teeth. It could have been a man or a woman or both.

I can't move easily because I'm a newborn baby. I see my little hands closed in pink fists and the new skin under my tiny feet. I put a hand in my mouth and lick every finger with my tongue. The black figure picks me up and I feel safe. I still can't see the face but I don't care and close my eyes.

When I open them again I am much taller than the wooden table. I'm still cold and I see the same puff from my mouth and when I hear the click of the door fear rises from my legs up to my back and my shoulders and I need to hide. The black figure is coming down the stairs and I hide under the table even though I know it's useless. A name I don't recognize is called in the air but I know it's mine. I've been betrayed by whoever called that name and I'm angry about it. I'm betrayed and powerless and I'm now out from under the table. The black figure is just stepping down from the last step, ready to come closer. I want to run away but can't possibly find the strength in my heart. So I stay and when the figure comes closer I'm now standing up and looking at the table. And I'm on the table myself and I stabbed my other self with the knife. I don't feel any pain but I see a mist coming out from my body on the table.

And I'm the one on the table and I see the black figure's face.

It's Mallory.

She puts her hands into the wound in my belly and I don't feel any pain. When she takes her hands out she has a little golden chain tied to her wrist at one end, while the other end is going into my navel and to me. That feels normal. I have the feeling she could rip my soul away just by pulling the chain out. I try to pull the chain towards myself but nothing happens.

Then my entire body is lifting up and I start ascending faster and faster into the white.

eight

The light was strong and it took me a couple of blinks and squints to get accustomed to it. Without moving my head, I looked around. White walls. One large window. A door in front of me. White sheets.

Paradise looked a lot like a hospital room.

I felt something in my left arm and I moved slightly and the pain hit me hard. A hospital room. Pain. I was stabbed. I remembered. I was in a hospital room in a bed with a beeping machine next to me and tubes with one end in my left arm and dripping bottles at the other. My right hand had a little clip on the pointing finger. I touched my face with my right hand. No beard. I hadn't been there for weeks. That was a good thing. Or maybe I had and they'd shaved me. I moved slowly to sit up a bit and learned that if I avoided twisting I could move without too much pain. I slid a bit up the pillows and looked around more carefully.

On the right was a door with a glass panel at the very top, maybe the way out. Next to the bed, a chair and a blanket. Someone had slept there. On the bedside, a half-eaten sandwich. Someone was still here. Neil's dead; it can't be him. I felt my temperature rising from the inside of my guts up to my cheeks in a flash and the beeping machine started beeping more rapidly.

Mallory. Mallory was here. The girl I'd trusted. The girl who stabbed me. I looked around for a button to call the nurse; I twisted and let out a yelp of pain. I raised the blanket to check and looked inside the white gown. My body was bandaged, two little red dots sprouting from the white.

The noise of a toilet flushing came from the door in front of the bed. I tried to move but couldn't, so I only slid up a little more. The door opened and out of it came Death, wiping his hands on his black skinny pants. I couldn't contain myself and shrieked,

What!

Hello, boy. You are awake. Good to see you. He came towards the chair and picked up the sandwich half.

I tried covering myself with the blanket to find protection from him.

Do you mind if I finish that? I hate skipping breakfast, he said, while biting the bread.

No, I don't—oh. Oh my god. I get it. I didn't realize I'm dead.

No, my boy, you are alive.

I am?

Yes, you are.

What the fuck are you doing here?

Oh, that is nice. No thanks for being at your side, huh?

At my side?

Yes. Who do you think stayed here for two nights while you were flying high on morphine? Your ghost friend? He took another bite of the sandwich then opened a can of soda.

Neil's still here? What about Mallory?

Death's face became serious, as he spoke. Mallory. That girl is something, I tell you. She has courage. Are the two of you together?

No. I don't think so. We've been together. Why is that important? Where is she?

The heck if I know, my boy. I am asking you.

This time, I realized his voice was different. It sounded like a normal voice, the voice of a single person. Still with a touch of foreign accent though, and still formal. I continued,

Where is she?

I told you. I do not know. We will work on this.

Aren't you Death? Aren't you supposed to know where people are?

That is funny. You are telling me how to do my job. I tell you, do not annoy me again, boy. It is already enough to have lost at chess for the first time since - he paused and looked up - *eternity*.

Lost at chess? I could feel the incredulity in my eyes, getting bigger.

Yes. A dull game, if you ask me. If your girl had not distracted me, that would not have happened. Well, that is how it goes; I cannot blame others for my losses.

Is that why I'm alive? Because I won?

Do not be silly! You are alive because the paramedics were swift at giving you first aid, and because the doctor did not need explorative surgery. It was a clean cut.

But I won.

Yes, you did. We have established that. He seemed really irritated.

So that means Neil is alive as well?

He stopped eating. He put the sandwich on the bedside. No, he said. He is still dead.

But.

No but, my boy. He is dead and dead he will stay.

Didn't you say I won?

You did.

So you owe me. I couldn't believe the words coming from my mouth, especially knowing who was receiving them on the other end.

I owe you, eh?

I guess.

He looked towards the window. I suppose you are right.

A smile appeared on my face. Where's Neil? I said.

I do not know.

You don't know.

I think you have hearing problems.

You'll bring him back.

That is not something I can do. It is not how it works.

Then how does it work?

Listen, he said, leaning from his chair towards my bed. I might not be dressed as a scary skeleton, but that is not how it works. That is not how *you* work, he said, pushing his finger into my chest—two inches down and I would have screamed in pain. He leaned back on the chair. I do not make the rules, he added.

Who does then?

He was silent.

I was silent.

Also, you won because you cheated. Your pretty girlfriend did something strange and interrupted me. I should consider it a foul game.

I kept my mouth shut.

Now you are not talking. I like that.

He finished the sandwich with a last bite and started playing with the crumbs on the nightstand, moving them around, creating shapes and then breaking them apart and creating new ones.

My eyes were mesmerized by his hands, and the beeping machine slowed. I was falling asleep again and my last conscious thought was that we are just little crumbs in the hands of Death.

When I woke up another day had passed. A nurse told me they were cutting down on the painkillers so I might feel more pain, but I'd be able to leave the hospital soon. Where to, that was up to me. In the space of one week I'd witnessed the death of my best friend, met a girl who made my heart sink but almost killed me, and discovered the existence of realms beyond what we know. Oh, and drank enough to sink a ship.

Death was sitting on the chair.

Hey.

Hello, boy.

So.

Here we are.

Did Neil show up?

No.

Huh.

I believe he is still with your female friend.

You believe so.

I do not know if he followed her on purpose because of what she did, or if she managed to *bind* him and bring him with her.

Why would she do that?

People have their reasons, he said, and stood up. His anthropomorphic incarnation was definitely just skin and bones.

What could she possibly want from Neil?

Or from you, he said.

From me? What do you mean?

Well, she stabbed you for her ritual. She must have wanted something. He paused and looked up, with his long fingers resting on his chin. Did you have any weird dreams? He asked.

I actually did. How did you know?

He smirked.

Nevermind.

What did you dream? he asked.

I don't remember it very well. Just a weird feeling. And Mal. Doing something with my blood. The binding ritual must have gone bad, I guess.

He sat down with a serious face, then said, Blood, huh? And a binding ritual, eh? It seems like she managed to bind something after all.

What did she manage to bind? You?

Oh, again you are so silly! I am talking about you.

Me? How did she bind me?

You, your spirit, or soul. Call it what you want. She—he paused, looked up, looked for the word—how can I say it? *Connected* with you.

Is that even possible?

Is seeing ghosts or talking to the incarnation of Death possible?

Good point. I guess you're right then.

I am. I always am.

So what do I do now? I should call the police!

You can, of course. But I would suggest a different approach.

And what would that be?

I suggest we go after her, find her, and you make her reverse whatever it is that she did. Embarking on the police route might be an impediment to reversing her spell, or whatever it was that she did.

We? I said and pushed the button to raise the bed. Now I was almost sitting.

You did beat me at chess.

Yes.

I cannot bring your friend back. I can help you find him though, and find the girl.

Thank you. I guess.

Then I will go on my way. Do you have any clue where she might be?

Can't you just locate her?

I am not a GPS. I do not know where she is.

I drank from the glass of water and started muttering words that died before turning into meaningful phrases.

What? Death said.

Nothing.

Come on.

I mean, you're Death, right?

I am indeed.

How come you can't find someone? I said, and took another sip, to hide my face.

Potentially, I could.

Then do it!

It is not that easy.

Why?

Because I am not *her* Death.

What?

Everyone has their own Death, remember? Sometimes someone shares one, sometimes a crowd shares one. But everyone has their own. I am yours.

Mine?

While you are here, boy, you should really have them check your hearing.

What do you mean *mine*?

Not that you possess me. But that I am your Death. I always know where you are. I am always with you. Since your birth.

How many of you are there?

As many as needed, he replied.

Do they all, do they all look like you?

Some might. Everyone figures it out by themselves. It might be the trash man in the early morning or the newspaper salesman in the evening. The barista behind the counter. Any of them. You don't truly know until the end.

All the time?

Yes.

Until the end.

Until the end. The end is what you really care about, is it not? Well, I say that if you really cared about it, you would have thought more about it. Prepared yourself.

Prepared? Like, how?

Being kind, first of all. How many times do you say hello to the trash man? Smile at the barista? Do you nurture your relationships? Do you nurture your Death? Because the way you nurture it will matter a great deal about the way you will die.

What about Neil? Are you his Death as well?

Not quite.

So how did he die?

The same way as many people. His heart died first, and he followed. Remember?

I do. But I mean, where was his Death?

Next to me.

For a split second my forehead wrinkled, but then I exclaimed The crow!

Yes.

So the crow is another Death?

Yes. It was supposed to guide Neil.

But why did I see it?

That is a very good question. You and Neil were close friends.

Yes.

Feelings bond people. They create empathy. That is all it takes. Compassion and empathy. So you and Neil are connected, and that is why you were witnessing not only his material Death, but also why you had a glimpse of what happened. On other levels.

I see.

Once that was important. Being truly connected with other people. It was an age when the dreams of your people were full of heroes and fairies; they've gone rotten now.

Are you giving me advice?

You asked for it.

I sat in the bed, silent.

You sleep now. We will be out of here soon. We need to find that Mallory of yours.

He walked towards the door and said I am going to get another sandwich. It was rather good. Do you want something?

I shook my head. What can Mallory possibly do?

We will talk about it. Now you sleep.

Thanks, Death.

He paused on his way out and turned towards me. He smiled and said,

You can call me D.

One more day and I was ready to get out of the hospital. D stayed by my side the entire time. It wasn't easy to have a conversation with him. I asked many questions, and the only answer I would receive was *We will talk about it.* When? *When it will be the right time.*

The only topic he would touch was Neil's death. Not the event itself or our meeting. He just kept saying to me *This is what happens when you do not let go. You do not let go and people are not here, but not there.*

He didn't tell me what this *there* was. *We will talk about it later*, he said.

The nurse came to check my bandages one last time. They gave me some painkillers for the next few days. I was ready to go. I signed out. I collected my stuff and left. When I got to my car, D was at the wheel. I didn't ask if he knew how to drive or *how* he knew how to drive or if he even had a driving license. What name would be on that license, anyway? He drove straight to my place, smoothly. I felt like we'd known each other for a long time. And that was true in part. All my life I've known that I'd die. Eventually.

What now? I said.

You go in. Collect some clean clothes. Then we move.

Move where?

We need to find Mallory. You know where she lives.

I do.

We will check there first. See if she is at home. See if we find anything.

Good thinking.

Thank you.

In my apartment, I emptied the duffel bag onto the floor and filled it up again with t-shirts and pants and underwear and socks. I took a jacket from the closet. Then I thought *Why am I packing?* Mal's house was only four hours away, give or take. Were we going to stay someplace? I took two pairs of sunglasses and zipped the bag shut. I went into the bathroom to get my toothbrush and then I saw it. Almost hidden behind the toilet was a small, round object. I recognized it immediately. An old pocket watch.

Neil's watch. An object to cling to, to remember my friend. The police didn't see it, or didn't care, apparently. I put it in my pocket and felt better. Ready to go.

Back in the car I handed one pair of sunglasses to D. He closed his hands together on the glasses. He opened the two arms out and turned them to look at them from different angles.

It's for the sun, I said. You can't really see if you're driving and it's that sunny.

Thank you. Really.

No problem.

Sunglasses, he said curiously.

He put them on, and started the car. The song *Don't Fear the Reaper* by Blue Oyster Cult started blaring from the ancient stereo and I swear that I saw his eyes – a reddish hue reminiscent of flames - *winking* at me from behind the sunglasses.

nine

Driving south always gave me the feeling that it was the trip and not the destination that matters. And the last time I'd done it I'd had to keep all thoughts out of my mind so I wouldn't drift apart in sorrow. The cut in my gut wasn't only physical, and with my best friend dead and a girl who was probably sneaking around under my skin at that very moment, I found myself surprised at enjoying the road, the stream that flows when you're going someplace, the warm thought of a destination. The sun burning my skin.

I was enjoying it because I was alive. One day I'll be dead, but that day wasn't it.

When we had a good few miles behind us, we stopped for a bite in a diner. I ordered a cup of coffee. D asked for the same. I looked at the menu. A thought hit me, so I put down the menu for a second and asked,

Do you eat?

I am looking at the menu right now, he replied.

Yes, but I mean, do you usually eat?

I do not.

Oh.

Yes. But I am going to eat now. Even if this place is not a *gourmet* one, is it?

It's an on-the-road stop. You can't be picky.

I want a cinnamon pancake.

We ate our meal and drank our coffee in silence. We paid and left.

Do you want me to drive? I asked.

No, I will be fine driving.

Alright.

It is just that I do not do it that often, you know.

No problem. I'll just relax.

We drove south for fifty miles on the freeway, passing town after town. At a certain point I couldn't keep quiet anymore. *We'll talk about it now*, I thought, and said,

D.

Yes, boy?

So, *what* are you?

Death.

I think I know that. But I mean, what exactly is death then?

We will talk about it later.

No. There's no later. I don't want to wait until the end.

He looked at me. I could see his eyes behind the sunglasses. Okay. You can ask your questions now, he said.

I felt excitement building and couldn't keep my hands still. I don't know where to start!, I said - Is there a God?

You mean a bearded man with a white robe, up in the clouds, who created everything and supervises heaven and hell?

Yes? That's the man. Is he there?

Do you want him to be?

What? Is that an answer? Come on.

I am serious. It is not a matter of whether God exists or not, it is a matter of whether you need him to exist or not.

I need to know if he exists.

What would that change? Would you behave differently?

I believe so.

Well, start to behave differently then. You do not need anything up above to be who you want to be.

I stayed quiet for a second. Then looked at him. You didn't really reply, I said.

I replied to the best of my ability.

So there's no God.

I never said such a thing.

Aha! So there is!

You make your own reality. If you want God to be there, you will find him.

I don't understand this at all.

Your people have tried to understand it since the beginning of time and they are still far behind, if you want my opinion. Do not wrap your head too much around such thoughts, as they are not useful.

But then who created everything?

What if everything was here before? he replied.

Where were you before?

I was here when *you* were here. And that should be enough.

I was silent. D looked at me and moved his lips up in a sympathetic grin.

I will try to explain it to you. It is hard. I will do my best, but I will not repeat myself. Understood?

Sure. I leaned towards him, like a kid listening to a good story.

Take the universe. You know what *that* is, right?

Yes, I suppose.

Excellent. The universe is what you observe, even if you are only seeing a tiny part of it. To observe this part, you decompose it into multiple parts, and to measure those parts, you use time. When you take all those single particles of time and put them together, you have the feeling of time flowing. Because that is all you see, time for you is everything and flows from beginning to end. This is how you perceive yourself, as well. Are you following, my boy?

Huh. More or less. I think. Maybe.

I will make it easier, then. You perceive yourself as a single part. But your self is the sum, or bundle, of all the parts of time you have experienced. The continuity of this makes up the narrative of your life. Your self is the sum of all the selves that experienced the single, bare moment of existence. As you perceive yourself as this particular narrative and you experience time flowing in one direction, you have a beginning and an end. Thus, you call the part of time you experience *existence* and everything else you call *non-existence*. But there is no self, and there is no existence.

So I'm not really myself, or something?

More or less.

What am I then?

Only you can know. No one can tell.

I think I just want to know if I'm going to die. Like, non-exist.

Were you listening? Time is a human concept.

I get that, but then what about ghosts? Neil?

Look at it like an *echo* of the remaining self. I told you.

You told me I clung to him.

Yes. Your desire to keep your friend with you made his—let us call it, sum of narrative — stay here. He must have done his part as well, if you want my humble opinion.

What's supposed to happen then?

We will find out. But don't you worry with metaphysical conundrums - we have a task at hand that is more important now, and that is to find the girl.

Find the girl. Then what?

Then we slap her on the hand for playing with stuff that does not belong to her.

And then?

Then we probably have a counseling session and see if Neil can let go of you and if you can let go of him, and we will all be merry.

I slid down in the seat and crossed my arms. I still have questions you know, I said.

I know. I am answering.

But I don't understand a thing.

That is not my fault then, is it?

Very funny.

Alright, for the last time, I will try. Do not be sad. There's no abyss. You might not understand the mechanics behind it. He paused, looking for words. He tapped twice with his fingers on the cockpit, and said, It's like a car: You do not know how the engine works, but you do not care, as long as it takes you where you need to go. Right? Right. Then look at life the same way. It is a journey whose mechanics you do not need to understand. You probably *cannot* understand. Does that make sense to you?

I didn't know whether to nod or not. I nodded.

You are bound to experience things in such small portions of space and time; however, this is powerful enough. You are among the only beings who *know* they are alive. Not in a simplistic, sense of survival fashion. You understand that you have one life and you ask yourselves questions and you feel and suffer and love and gaze upon the boundaries of existence. You sit on a rock revolving around a star—*a mote of dust suspended on a sunbeam.* You are the final byproduct of thousands of millions of years. You are the most complex thing the universe engineered. You are what makes sense of the chaos, you are the order of things. Let me put it this way, he said. *You* - and he paused for a second before looking me in the eyes - are the meaning of life.

ten

It took us three more hours of freeway driving through flatlands and crops and deserts before we finally arrived. The town appeared almost immediately. I didn't ask D any more questions. I already had enough on my plate to eat and digest. He said a couple of other things while I kept quiet, like the universe recycles everything: plastic; glass; bodies - souls. And that he was sorry if he was unable to explain things in terms I could understand. He said that in the end it didn't matter.

So? Can you drive us to her house? D said.

I don't know. I think so. I was drunk, and with my head someplace else. Take a right here.

We took another right and after half a mile we went left and I recognized the road. We found it. Mal's house was at the end of a small lane. From the outside it looked like no one was there, so I asked,

What now?

Well, now you go and knock on the door.

Me? She stabbed me, remember?

It is not the stabbing we are worried about, right?

What is it that we are worried about then?

Oh, nothing terribly important. Just your soul.

I adjusted myself in the seat so I could look right at him. Why do you think my soul is in danger?

Let me see. Because a girl performed a strange ritual on you and you are having dreams of her with her hands in your guts? If I were you, or simply mortal, I would be worried.

That was just a dream. And, by the way, how do you know about that particular bit? I didn't even remember that myself.

Perks of the job, I guess. And dreams are never just dreams.

What does that mean?

Whatever you experience in your life, you experience through your senses. Dreams are behind the scenes, the backstage of the world where you can go while asleep. And while there you know all the scenes and all the actors because you're not on stage anymore. Dreams are signs and hints of the fact that you *are* more. That everything that was, is, and will be has been done. Just not yet.

I looked at D and said, Summarizing then - she can hurt me in my dreams.

That is a very simplistic way of putting it and not entirely correct, but if it makes you understand it, yes, she can.

So I go and knock and tell her to undo whatever it is she's done.

And do not forget to say please.

I gave a short laugh. No, I won't forget to say please to the woman who stabbed me.

It is important to be polite.

I shook my head and got out of the car. The air was chilly and smelled like dust. The sun was warming everything it touched. I walked to the door in a very different frame of mind than the one before. I knocked. No one answered. I knocked again. *Mallory? Guess who's here.* No reply. I took my cell phone out and tried to call her. Her phone was dead.

What should we do? I said to the car with D inside.

Well, we are sure that no one is inside. And you are sure that this is indeed her house, are you?

I am.

I say we open the door and go in.

We tried the door, but it was locked. We walked around the house and tried the back door. We've learned that the doors that are destined to open are always unlocked and this was, again, one of them. The handle clicked and we were in.

The house looked the same, like no one had been here since she and I left. D wandered around. He skipped the occult books. He was more fascinated by other things—the color of the pillows, the arrangement of the pictures. The faces in the pictures.

Who is this man? D said, taking up a photograph from the desk.

I came closer. I don't know. It looks a bit like her.

It might be her father.

It might.

And this woman with this golden pendant here?

I don't know. Her mother?

It looks like her mother. What a fragile creature. He put the picture back. Is Mal an only child?

Actually, no. She told me that she has a sister. A twin, to be precise.

D spun around and threw his hands up in the air, while saying, And you only tell me now?

Is it that important?

His face glowed. Of course it is! Twins share so many things that they might well share dreams and deaths.

So if we find her-

If we find her sister we might be lucky and she might point you in the right direction. She might share the same *passions*, shall we say, as her sister.

I hope not. I don't want to get stabbed again.

Be careful what you wish for. Also, she might be useless. But we will not know until we find her. We should go at once. Do you know where this sister is?

That's funny. She's in Vegas.

And why is that funny?

Because she works as a stripper, I said.

How do you find this funny?

I mean, it's not *funny* funny. It's weird, that's all.

It is her fate, you mean?

No, I just mean—nevermind.

What is her name? Do you know it?

It was something like Angela. No, Angelene.

That is good news. We have a name and a city. And I have never been to Vegas.

I sat down on the couch. But it could take us forever to find her!

Why are you so pessimistic? How many strippers named Angelene do you think there are in Las Vegas?

You don't have a clue about Vegas, do you?

And you probably have no clue as to how serendipity works. Trust me; to Vegas we shall sail.

We beat on, checking the house for a clue that might help us narrow our search. Apparently, there was no ongoing communication between the sisters. If they were identical twins, I was sure we'd be able to recognize Angelene easily. But Las Vegas was full of dancers and people and lost souls. And if Mallory turned out to be a stabbing bitch, I was more than a little worried about what her sister might be capable of. Eventually we found envelopes, addressed to Mallory Day. It was better than nothing. Unless it turned out to be a fake name. This time I got into the driver's seat.

It's a long trip to Vegas, I said.

Yes, sir. We will take turns. I could drive all the time, but I suppose taking turns is what friends do.

I looked at him and smiled. I might not understand how all that stuff works, D, but there's one thing I think I got right.

And what would that be?

You're not a bad guy.

He smiled and put on his sunglasses.

eleven

The road in the desert is plain and straight for miles and miles and you can't really see the ending so you feel like you're going to drive forever. We stopped once for gas, but other than that we kept the wheels turning. The sun set and we drove in the beginning of the night. You could see the stars even from inside the car, and everything around was just dark shapes against dark sky. Suddenly the heart of this darkness would crack on the horizon, with beams of lights from buildings sprung out of nowhere, like an abandoned spaceship that forgot how to fly and was just sitting there, inviting you in. Those were the last towns before Vegas, which appeared like a gleaming, endless blanket of crawling lights in the desert. We drove in to the streets where all things were created to give the illusion of faraway lands. Pyramids and metal towers and canals and ruins. Waves and currents of human beings, circling inside an open-air fishbowl, driven only by the desire of *sleeping 'til late, having fun, getting wild.*

We took just a couple of unconventional turns and left the lights behind, plunging into unexplored land, where locals would look at you like you're not a person but an object, something to squeeze out, to drain, to fuck and kill and love and hurt and kiss. Because that is the terrible human need to feel alive, and sometimes letting yourself go to the darkness of the soul is easier than trying to understand what is different.

These were the people that chose to make this city their home. I wondered what had driven Mal's sister here. Whether she was anything like her twin. Whether she was selfish and evil and had deep, beautiful eyes to get lost in.

We rolled around just enough and then decided to check in to a small, dirty, cheap motel right off the road. The room smelled like thousands of years. We had two beds and a shared bedside table in the middle. I opened the drawer to empty my pockets: coins; roll of bills; wallet; sleeping pills; Neil's watch. I took the Gideon bible out of the drawer and left it there on the stand. I went to the bathroom to take a shower and let go of some thoughts. This part of the trip had been rough so far. The road was smooth, but the path in my heart wasn't. I felt a hole in my chest and the glooming feeling of something terrible about to happen. Like something terrible hadn't already.

When I came out of the shower D wasn't in the room anymore. No note. I dressed quickly and headed to the lobby. Behind a computer screen I saw D. I came closer. He was checking suit rentals.

We will need suits if we have to go from casino to casino, he said.

I think just a jacket will do.

I thought you had to be well dressed.

Nah. Just a jacket. Trust me. We'll pick one tomorrow. One for me and one for you.

Oh, he said, and sighed.

What?

I would have liked to look different for once.

From the first moment I saw D, he was dressed in black, with skinny black jeans and black t-shirt. Apart from the moment of Neil's demise, and Mal's ritual, where I saw him in his *uniform,* so to say, black was the only color I've seen on him. It wasn't normally easy to read his face – it looked like it had no definite expressions whatsoever, or a very definite one for a short moment, but so intense that you would use it as the archetypal face for that emotion. If I had to make a bet, the face he wore when he said he wanted to look different for once was *disappointment*. We left the computer screen open on a white tuxedo and went back to the room.

I didn't have the energy to go out in search of Angelene immediately, but I couldn't fall asleep either. My mind was racing. The emotional pain was dripping slowly into my bones. My entire body ached. I lied on the bed and tried to focus my mind on something else. The stain on the ceiling looked like a painting out of some Romantic painter – the pit of souls, contorting and screaming to be saved. The perfect *pareidolia* to have in that moment. When my breathing calmed down, all the pain, sorrow and thoughts started to make me drowsy. I asked the air, not really expecting an answer,

What are the chances?

What? D replied.

That we'll find this girl. I mean, Vegas is the city of strippers.

Exotic dancers. I believe they prefer that name.

Whatever. It's statistically impossible.

If you add up the volumes of all the bodies in the solar system and compare it with the total volume of the system itself, it turns out that *statistically* nothing exists. 99.9995 percent of the solar system is empty space.

Great, I replied.

And with that thought, my body fell asleep.

I'm walking down a big street. Wide trees are branching out from both sides. The more I walk, the narrower the road gets. I can see the first lights of the sun coming from behind the trees and I know it's dawn. Everything in the sky is golden and I feel summer heat on my skin. I know there are birds in the trees, but they're silent, too tired from the scorching heat. I smell the air and it's full of perfumes that I can't really recognize, but that are pleasant to me. I keep walking and smelling the air and suddenly - a wave of joy rises in my body; I could walk for miles and miles without getting tired. So I keep walking. The road starts to be populated with beautiful girls. All of them wear nothing but their skin. Naked. My task is to cover them, as their beauty is wasted on the eyes. In my hands are pieces of white cloth. I give them to the naked girls and they smile at me and thank me and they wear them.

All the girls I'm dressing now dance before my eyes. At every turn of their eyes they smile at me and caress my face. These girls are all the beauties of the world. And they're dancing for me. And I know that if I stop I could stay here in these woods of flesh forever, but I hear a voice—no, feel a voice inside me, calling my name. So I keep walking and handing out pieces of white cloth that turn into full clothes as soon as the girls put them on.

I follow the voice; my hands are empty. But in front of me, far away at the end of the lane, I see one last naked body. And even though she's far away I know she's the most beautiful one. I know it by the smell and the sound of her. I know by the taste that I already feel in my mouth. So I start running towards this beauty but the more I run, the further away she is. I keep running towards her and then I turn and I see that a small golden chain keeps me from reaching her. I try to break free, break the chain with my bare hands, but I can't. I look at her and she also has a chain that runs in the same direction as mine, and they're connected at a third point that I can't see.

I keep running towards her, running towards her, running towards her.

twelve

We left the hotel as soon as we woke up. I wasn't hungry – I didn't remember any of my dreams, but I had that feeling like you've been working all night instead of sleeping, so we didn't stop for breakfast. Instead, we looked for a store where we could find a couple of elegant piece of clothing, just to be able to end up in better places than the dodgy ones. We went to a place that sold suits, shirts, and tuxedos. I took the first blazer I found, black and anonymous. D was shuffling an endless rack of black suits. I saw a white breasted suit on the tall man rack, moved to grab it, and brought it to D. When he saw the suit his red eyes widened and a smile appeared on his face.

Do you think I can?, he said.

I nodded.

We were ready to start our search. Whenever you need to look for something but you don't know where to start, any point is a good point, so we walked into the first casino we came across. Wandering around in that modern Babylon left us drained of any sense of time—every building carefully crafted to make people think the night of youth is eternal. Lights were beaming colored dots on the ceiling while rhythmic bass entered your bones, shattering any thought – music built to trigger animal instincts, to relieve the mind from the burden of itself.

As much as I normally would've enjoyed watching naked girls on poles, I wasn't in the mood. The hole in my chest was taking up every other feeling I had. I felt my energy slip out of me each time I inserted a bill into yet another small piece of clothing of yet another twentysomething girl. It was a disheartening task, talking with dancers in the middle of a gig. They would utter a sound only after a conspicuous rain of dollars; ineffective and expensive, and I wasn't really swimming in gold. For a second, I thought about how much money we had left. I had some savings, but this trip was eating dangerously into them. One of the girls I was watching right now noticed my blank stare – thinking about my bank account while her body was beautiful in front of me – and came closer to grab my eyes and direct them to her naked chest.

Some of them were very beautiful. For every dollar I laid at their feet or in their clothes, I laid a gentle thought as well. I wondered about their dreams—if they'd dreamed of this life when they were just little kids. I wondered if dancing naked for other people made them feel powerful or beautiful or fragile. I wondered what kind of drinks did they like. What kind of books. What poets, if any, moved their soul. Would they dream better dreams than me? Would they eat pancakes in the morning, and smile and be fragile? I wondered at normal life. I wondered what pajamas they wore.

Some of them were half naked and some of them were totally naked; all of them wore a mask. Because no one can wear their heart completely naked. Endless are the buffers that shield the heart from the body.

In my mind I played a little game, I'd materialize white dresses on them and sandals and imagine them walking on a shore at sunset shuffling feet in the sand, hand in hand with their lovers. I wondered if that's what they were searching for when they came here. Every search is the search for happiness. I wondered what they'd found and why they were staying.

Throwing bills at girls didn't suit me, so we tried another way. We thought it might be easier to fish for information directly from the bartenders. The managers. But no one knew any Angelene, although many offered to give us girls who'd let us call them by any name.

We finished another drink as the night was turning into early morning and we went back to the motel. Turns out D didn't really need to sleep, of course. He would lie still in bed, eyes closed, in what looked like deep meditation. But he wasn't sleeping. He was probably just making me comfortable by doing something that looked more human.

I slipped into a clean t-shirt and dropped onto the bed. In the silence of the room my ears were replaying echoes of the music, and the reel of naked bodies under my eyelids didn't let me rest. I sat on the side of the bed and took a pill from the bottle. I turned on the small lamp. The Bible was on the stand.

I opened it and read the first line that caught my eye.

And in her was found the blood of prophets, and of saints, and of all that were slain upon the earth.

D was standing on the bed, looking at me. What was strange was that I didn't even find this odd. I muttered a lazy *Good morning* and checked the time. It was already late and this time I was starving. I got dressed and we went to grab something to eat, choosing the first open bar that served food. Once inside, it was the eternal night all over again. The dancing poles and the high-rise stages, orphans of their night queens, seemed like rafts ashore after having travelled on a sea of bodies during a storm. We ordered food and made plans for the day—which strip bar to check, which agencies to call to see if they offered private dancers, and maybe, just maybe, one of their dancers would be named Angelene. I handed my card to the waiter to settle the bill. He came back with a long face.

Declined, sir.

I tried again. Declined again.

Fuck.

What?

The card. It's maxed out. Fuck!

What does that mean?

It means we're out of money. Here, I said, and gave a one hundred-dollar bill to the waiter.

He came back with the change. I counted what I had. One hundred-sixty dollars and change. That was it. That was all the money we had. I panicked. There was nothing I could do. I just wanted to go home. D looked at me.

I shouldn't do this, he said.

What?

Come with me, and trust me.

We walked out of the bar and onto the street. The heat of the afternoon was unbearable. D started walking.

Where are you going?

I told you. Trust me.

If you know where we're going we could take a cab. It's too hot to be walking around. I'm melting.

I thought that is the last of your money.

It is.

I always despised this buy-things-sell-things system. But I suppose it is necessary. No one will notice, anyway.

What do you mean? I was seriously confused.

I told you to trust me. Give me the money.

I gave him the money. I followed him along the whole length of the road, until we skipped a couple of turns and reached a street with holes in the ground and litter on the side and homeless people hiding in ATM rooms. D kept walking and I kept following. We got to a small square, more of a parking lot. There was a garage door. A short, bulky man wearing a black t-shirt and a thin mustache was outside it, sitting on a chair and sipping from a bottle hidden in a brown bag.

How much to enter? D asked the guy.

Who sent you?

How much?

Twenty bucks. D looked at me and I gave the guy two bills and the guy knocked on the garage door.

What are we doing? I whispered. He didn't reply.

The inside of the garage was something like an open space casino. From the look of the people inside, the weird bouncer outside - it wasn't a regular one. Girls were walking around completely naked, except for little aprons and cowboy hats. Some of them were young and ugly and some of them were older and smelled of tobacco and alcohol and some of them were fat and loud. I doubted we'd find Angelene anywhere near the place. I wondered how D knew the place. I followed him, zig-zagging around and getting to the far end of the room, where at a table with a green, stained cloth three people were shuffling cards. One of them was a young Japanese guy with shorts and no shoes and facial hair too sparse to actually call it a beard. The other two were white guys, one in his forties with only a strand of hair on his head and a huge belly, and the other dressed in worn-out classic pants, brown shoes, and a very thin mustache. He could have been anywhere between thirty and fifty.

Mind if we join you?

They smiled at us, the fat guy showing a fake golden tooth.

I'm terrible at cards, D! I whispered.

Do not worry, my boy. You beat me at chess; you can beat them at cards.

We sat down. They started shuffling again. We started playing.

I didn't beat anyone and almost immediately lost the few bills I had left, but D won the first three rounds without a problem. I was flabbergasted. In the space of a few minutes he changed our financial outlook considerably, winning something in the range of five hundred dollars. Two men looked at each other and signaled a third. The third man nodded and disappeared behind a curtain. When he was back he had a bottle of whiskey with him. He sat down and opened the whiskey, poured three glasses, and gave one to each of the players. D refused his and gave it to me. I took the glass. The man who brought the whiskey got rid of his jacket and stayed at the table to join the game. D won again, and again. And again. The four men started shouting and screaming and accusing us of cheating. I guess you don't beat Death unless you cheat.

Or, unless he wants you to.

D kept calm and gathered up the bills. He paid for the whiskey and we left a good tip for the girls who came to calm down the men. We could hear them still shouting *cheater!* the whole way back through the casino. D smiled at the entrance guy and we slipped him another twenty. Then we raised our hands and a cab stopped and we entered the car, finally shielded from the heat of the city, from the heat of the people.

How did you do it? I asked.

When you feel like you do not know what to do, you just have to have faith and let go.

I mean, how did you win?

Oh that! I like games, remember?

I wonder if I would have ever beaten you if it weren't for Mal.

You would not have had to play if it were not for Mal.

How much did you win?

Just enough to finish the trip and go home.

Can't we do it more often? Are other people doing this kind of thing?

You mean, cheating?

I mean what you did in there.

He shrugged. That is cheating. And one can live with only so much of it.

I smiled. Let's go find this lady.

That's the spirit! Where do you want to go?

I leaned towards the driver. Where's the worst strip bar in Vegas?

The driver looked at me from the rearview mirror and said, You into kinky stuff? I can take you to my cousin.

Unless her name is Angelene, I'm not interested, I chuckled.

No, her name is Rita. She does stuff you won't forget, kiddo.

Thanks, but take us to the place where people who are desperate and without hope go, I said.

He looked at me with a funny face, then said, Yes, sir, if that's what you want.

The car moved slowly from lights to lights until we were out of the evening crowd. We got to a parking lot with old battered cars here and there. The street lamps were yellow and not bright enough to delete the darkness except for small spots. In front of the strip club there were mannequins dressed as Marilyn Monroe and Jimi Hendrix and an inflatable pool with a kid's swing hung over it. D looked at me and smiled.

What now? he said.

Now we go in and have a drink.

thirteen

A bell announced our entrance. The white neon lights made the place as bright as a grocery store. The man behind the counter said Hi, elbowing a naked girl sitting next to him, who was mindlessly playing with her phone. She turned to send him off, but he nodded in our direction, so the girl started to look more alive.

I looked around. Shelves full of old DVDs were randomly placed in the middle of the big room and encompassed the world of everything pornographic. The naked girl put down her phone and stood up. She wore only a thong and high black heels and a white smile on an orange tanned face. She couldn't walk in the heels very well and with every step her knees would twist a bit. She wobbled her way towards us and took me under her arm, then said,

Hi, stranger.

Hi, you.

Name's Valerie; what's yours?

Lou.

Hi, Lou. Welcome to our club. Y'all been here before?

This would be my first time.

I'll make sure it's a good one.

She smelled like spray tan and soap and freshly washed blanket, which surprised me as pleasant – it was a nice change from the sea of human flesh I was now used to fighting through to talk to other strippers. We walked together towards a heavy, red curtain at the end of the shelves. There was a small, neatly dressed young man who welcomed us with the rules of the club, which were you can do anything and everything the girls want to do. And that's it. One weird move and you're out. We nodded and pushed through the curtain to the back.

Everything was darker here and my eyes took a moment to adjust. Valerie escorted us to a counter where we left ten dollars for the entrance and they gave us a complimentary drink. No alcohol allowed. I grabbed a soda and sat down in the back.

The counter was on our right and from where we were sitting we could see the whole room. Behind the counter was a doorway where the girls would come in and go out, which I assumed was the changing room. In the middle of the room was the only stage with a shiny copper pole and a girl dancing. It was the only well-lit spot. Everywhere else there were candles and small table lights that were just enough to animate a dance of shadows on the walls, but not enough to reveal the humans behind them. All around the central stage were tables and chairs and sofas. If I had to pick a color, I'd say everything was dark red. There were three men throwing bills at the dancer. One of them kissed a bill and waited for the girl to come close enough so he could tuck it into the last piece of clothing she had on. The dancer looked at the note and took off her thong and kept dancing, naked.

The place sort of reminded me of a Wild West brothel from the last century. That was the kind of feeling it gave off. Everything was worn out and had a lazy quality, and it was diametrically the opposite of the shiny new things that made up the city.

To me, this was the only place in Vegas that felt real.

I was still looking around and sipping my soda when a girl came over. She was wearing a bright bikini and heels and, in contrast with the bare *nakedness* of her body for sale, prescription glasses. Her smile was friendly and genuine. She waved to me, and when I waved back she sat on my lap, her arms across my shoulders.

Do you want a private dance? she asked.

I shook my head.

C'mon, you. Have some fun!

Thank you, but I'm looking for a girl - I couldn't finish as she interrupted me.

It looks to me you've found yourself one, she said, and kissed me on the cheek.

I smiled. Yes, I sure have. But the one I'm looking for is named Angelene. Do you know her?

She looked me in the eyes. You Angie's friend? She'll be up in no time.

I felt like someone spanked me on my back. I almost jumped out of my chair, and that was enough for her to lose her seat and fall on the floor with a loud cry.

I offered my hand to help her up, but she was mad. She wobbled away on her high heels and disappeared into the dark of the other side of the stage. I didn't care. We might have found her. We found her! I grinned at D. I had no time to voice my thoughts as the music stopped. I turned; the stage was now empty. A few customers started whistling and shouting. Then I heard a deep line of bass, and someone shouted something. From the dark hole that led to the stage I saw a figure emerging slowly, like a creature from the sea.

I couldn't see her yet, but I knew exactly who she was.

fourteen

A tidal wave, a flow of beauty, a goddess stood before me, emerged from the darkness of the pit; and if her face was unknown yet to my eyes, my heart was cut open by a splinter of her soul, a sort of metaphysical transfer of beings, a magical happening of a second.

The cloud of hair masking her face flowed left and right as she moved; but I did know her already, as I'd seen her in the dreams I've never had. Slowly, sumptuously, her sensual strut begun, and the time was frozen, and no one dared contaminate the air with words. A poet, give me a poet, my heart cried; for only a blessed soul could have described the being that treaded on the stage of my heart. And when she reached the center – golden calf, sinner and sin, deliver me from evil, keep me in your arms – the music started, and there was no bass and no bones to crush, no eyes to close but souls to touch, and a guitar started its cry, and with every chord and sound, the body of my goddess started her dance.

The golden snake took her body and moved her flesh, and all I could see was that gleam, an energy rising up from the bottom to the top, snake sinuously springing around her legs, her belly - sin and salvation; when suddenly her arms opened up and the cloud of hair shot to the sun, and a tempest took place inside me, and her breasts were the grapes of a forgotten summer and her belly was home to my sins and soul and her skin was a blanket for my heart. The volume increased, flowing like blood in my ears and I locked eyes with her for a moment, her hair dancing in the dark like horsetail fires, and the waves washed myself inside, and one with the eternal ocean I longed to be, oblivion to the eternal night.

And again and again and again, and again, she would turn her body and with every movement she turned my soul. There were no people around and no voices around and no places to be, because the entire world was now this woman, and she had all beauty within her, for if she were born when heroes walked the earth they would have burned cities for her, waged wars over her, as she herself was but a mirror in which to admire the eternal dance of the ephemeral order of things.

There in the scum I found peace and splendor; and I myself was forgotten.

I was *otherplace*, and there I would have stayed. So it took me a while to realize that the little guy, the one who let us in, was raining blows on my abdomen. My barely healed wound was registering shocks of pain. The girl with the glasses was giggling behind him. You dropped her, he said, and put a hand on the collar of my jacket and the other one in the back of my jeans and I tried to move his hands away, but he was a lot stronger than he looked.

I looked on stage, but she was gone; the spell was broken, the magic lost, I'd never be that pure again, as reality oozed in. Angelene finished her dance and the voices started up again and everything was normal and dull and covered in grime. I was now spectating the mundane, and found myself escorted off the premises by a semi-midget who was ten times stronger than me. He pushed me out of the door with a grin on his face and gave me the finger. I gave him the finger right back. I didn't care. We'd found Angelene, and I'd fallen in love.

fifteen

My feet were beating the asphalt in one direction for a while, then they would turn around and start again. Up and down the road, jumping from light to darkness to light again under the streetlights. I was worried someone might mug me. I wanted a cigarette badly—even though I didn't smoke. I wanted to go back in and stare at her and tell her I'd take her away with me, two thousand miles away. What was wrong with me? Up and down the road again. I didn't track how many minutes or hours or years passed while the night was running out. But eventually D came walking out the door.

So? I said, barely containing my excitement.

I would say we managed to find our lady.

Did you talk to her?

No.

No?

No.

Well then, now what? Do we come back every night until she notices us?

The lights on her are too strong; I do not think she is able to see the faces of her customers from up there.

I threw my hands up in the air.

And I asked for her phone number, but no one in this place would give it to me. They appear to be a respectable establishment.

I saw a cab coming down the street. Without thinking, I raised my hand and it stopped. I leaned towards the driver.

Hi. We have to wait for a friend here to finish her shift. Can you wait with us?

Do you have money?

Sure we do.

Jump in.

We opened the doors and sat down.

How long 'til your friend comes out?

Oh, just a few minutes, I replied. But maybe you should turn off the engine.

We waited. Ten minutes passed. At the fifteen-minute mark the driver wanted to see the money. We gave him a twenty and he shut up. After thirty minutes in silence, contemplating the red neon *Strippers!* going on and off and on and off he asked us what we were doing in town. Waiting for young ladies, D replied. More minutes passed. It was a dozen minutes shy of an hour when the taxi driver started to lose his temper. I'm wasting my time here, he said, and There'll be other cabs when your friend comes out.

And just then, in a white dress and white shoes, with her hair up in a bun, Angelene appeared at the back door. An angel risen from the mire. She dug her hands into her purse and out they came with a cigarette and a lighter. She lit it up. There she is, I said and the driver was about to turn the engine on. I stopped him. I took a note with the face of Benjamin Franklin and gave it to him.

We want to surprise our friend.

His eyes got bigger and he grabbed the bill with one hand. Without releasing it he looked at me and said Man, no funny business. You promise.

I nodded. I promise.

You not a killer or somethin' nasty?

I'm not. We're not.

He looked at me, then his eyes moved to D. His fingers felt the hundred dollars. I want double that, he said.

I shrugged. I released the first hundred. I took another hundred from my pocket and tore it in half. I gave him one half. The other half if you manage not to get us spotted, I said.

He looked at the ripped banknote, then at me, then at D, and then at Angie. She threw the cigarette on the ground and walked away from the *Strippers!* sign and towards an old car. The driver waited for her to turn the engine on and when she hit the gas we turned our engine on and we let her slide away for a couple hundred yards; we were watching her from afar. Even at that time of the night, or morning, there were people around and the city was alive. After a couple of miles the roads became darker and the people and cars and lights became scarce and then there wasn't much of anything.

We took a couple of turns and went out of the city, towards the desert. She turned right at a light and drove along a narrow road that ended in a residential estate with small, sand-colored houses. She parked in the driveway of one of the houses and turned the engine off. Just pass in front of it and come back, I told the driver. Angie turned for a second and watched the headlights coming and going. She turned her key in the lock and was in her house. What now? said the driver. Now we go home, I replied, and gave him the other half of the bill.

We knew where she lived.

The alarm on my phone went off after only a few hours of drugged and dreamless sleep. It was still early and we took the car and retraced the roads to her house. Her car was still in the driveway.

I wore sunglasses and a baseball hat and stepped out of our car. I looked at the house, wondering what to do next, how to approach her without looking like the creepy guy who stalked her home from her job. D rolled down the window and looked at me. Go talk to her, he said. I will be with you when you need me, he said. I walked up towards the door, then midway up I stopped and turned around. I wasn't sure what to do. I heard the click of a door and turned back and her door was open and she was out of it with a robe on and her hair up and no makeup and no heels and if I ever had a single thought that would have made sense to start the conversation, it disappeared in an instant.

Can I help you? Angelene said.

Hi. Hi. Yes, I think so. I actually believe you can, I replied.

She tightened her robe and walked backwards and half hid behind the door with a hand on the inside ready to shut it.

My name is Louis. I know your sister. Mallory.

She stood silent for a moment, then closed the door just enough to fit the chain. Are you with the police?

No, I'm not.

Is she dead?

I shrugged and widened my eyes and said, No, I don't think so.

Then I don't want to talk about her, she replied, and shut the door.

I looked at D, still in the car. He smiled and nodded encouragingly. I took a deep breath and walked to the door and knocked. Go away, her voice said. I knocked again. The door opened two or three inches, the length of the chain.

How'd you find me? she said. Did she send you?

Hi again. No, not exactly. I got your address from where you work.

Angelene looked at me like I supposed she would. A creepy man stalking the dancer home. So far, *not* very good.

Wait a second, I said. We're sorry to bother you, but we know about your *family gift*.

She tucked her hair behind her ear and looked at me. Her eyes were different than Mallory's. Deep and green and warm. But right now they looked puzzled. She said,

What are you talking about? Who are *we*?

Me and my friend there in the car, I said, and turned around. The car was empty. I looked around the yard. D wasn't there.

I think I should close the door.

No! Wait! I shouted, and then with a normal voice said, I need to find your sister.

And what made you think she'd be here?

You're her sister, I said. Maybe you know where she is.

I don't. You should go.

Wait, please. I joined my hands together. *Please*.

What? she said, and closed the door a bit more. The chain was now loose.

She has my brother, I said.

What the fuck are you talking about? I should call the police.

No. Please! Let me explain.

You don't have to. If your brother is missing, you should call the police, and I should close this door.

I can't call the police, I said.

Then I'm sorry, she replied, but I can still close the door.

And she closed the door.

I looked around. Turned towards the car. Empty. Kicked a small pebble. Then out of sheer frustration I shouted,

I can't call the police because my brother is dead. And he's not my brother, but my best friend and I don't care about blood or not, but he was a brother to me. And I'm sorry I lied. And now he's gone. And your sister messed with me and I need to find her. To make things right.

I sat on the doorstep and put my head in my hands. When my hands released my face back into freedom I looked around, but D hadn't come back. No one was there. I was alone. I sighed. Then I heard a sound from behind like metal sliding and rattling, and I turned. Angelene was holding the door open.

Come on in.

sixteen

The house of a goddess was different from expectations - perhaps an attempt to make her appear mortal when walking among us. Pieces of furniture inside the house were few and far between, and plain. A couch, a chair, a bookshelf with a few books. And the only other sign of someone living there was a photograph frame with a picture that looked like the family picture I saw at Mal's place. Too far away for me to see clearly. No television set, no phone. My eyes went back to the bookshelf. I was searching for a red flag—books with weird names or strange signs. I hoped not to get stabbed again. Sit, she said, and moved towards the small kitchen, divided from the hall only by a counter. Coffee? she said. I nodded. She poured me a cup. She came closer and sat on the couch next to me. Déjà vu. I hid my face in the cup and sipped. She broke the silence.

You said you were looking for Mal. With your friend. Where's he?

He was outside in the car. He must have left.

Good friend.

He's a bit weird, that's all.

Oh. Weirder than you? Following me home? She smiled.

I suppose so.

Then maybe it's better if he's not around. I can't handle two creeps at a time.

I'm not a creep.

See it from my side. You follow me home from work. Then you lie about your brother being dead and you claim to know my sister. What should I do? A normal person would call the police.

But you didn't call the police, did you? I felt a bit anxious.

Should I?

No.

Good. What's the story with my sister, then?

I sipped my coffee and took a moment to think. She'd flinched when I spoke about her family gift. Maybe that wasn't the right angle. So I told the true story, omitting the supernatural details – I told the story in a way that, if you read it in a newspaper, you would have believed it. I told her that my best friend died. That I met Mallory the night before the funeral. That I was sad and lonely and scared. That she wanted to help me. That she came with me to my apartment. That she hurt me and did something and took something of value from me—but what she could have possibly taken? Something that belonged to my friend. Something precious. If I had a stronger heart and a bolder mind, I would have said the whole truth, I would have confessed the secrets I knew. I would have said that she took my friend's soul and probably optioned mine, but we're made of matter and blood and ashes and we can never be bold with the invisible. So I just said,

She took something dear to me and she hurt me in the process. And I need to find her—we need to find her, me and my friend. So we thought to find her sister first. And eventually we did find you.

That you did.

And all the rest, too.

She stood up from the sofa and went to the kitchen to put the coffee cup in the sink. Her body moved with the same slow, mesmerizing pace that I remembered from the night before. A glimpse of magic seeping in the mudane again. She leaned on the counter.

Are you on any kind of medication? she said.

What? No! I've never been. Listen, you should talk to my friend. It'll be weird maybe, but then you'll believe me.

What did she take from you?

I can't tell you.

If you can't tell me, then all of this means nothing to me.

Let me find my friend. He can explain it better than I can.

Doesn't he have a phone?

A phone?

You know, those things you can use to call people.

A phone. Sure.

You can call him then. I can speak to him on the phone. Then I'll decide whether to call the police or not.

I took my phone out of my pocket and juggled with it for a moment. Call him, the voice in my head said. How could I call him? Angelene was looking at me. I fired up my contacts, already knowing I wouldn't find the direct line for the otherworld. I scrolled up and down and then decided. I tapped to call Neil. The call went straight to voicemail. I left a brief message saying that I was at Angelene's home, where the hell was he, that I needed him, that he needed to show up as soon as possible. The act of pretending to talk to a living being was only a masquerade to hide another stranger thing, the fact that while pretending to talk to Neil to fake a friend to call, I was praying, praying for possibly the only time in my life for Death to be next to me. I finished my hidden prayer and closed the call.

Voicemail? she asked.

Yes.

I see. Listen, I think you should go.

No! Please, just please. Help me.

She thought about it for a second or two, then shook her head. I can't help you, she said.

But you can help me find your sister! I shouted.

This must have scared her, because with a quick movement she took a small can out of her right pocket. It looked like a spray can of some sort.

What are you doing? I said.

Get out. Now. She stepped closer.

No, wait. Let's talk.

Get. The fuck. Out!

Wait. I moved closer. Let me show you something! Let me introduce you to my friend, you'll understand then!

If you take another step, I swear I'll spray you. And worse.

I stepped back. I started to lift my shirt, to show her where her sister had stabbed me. Bad move. Angelene jumped towards me like a cat and sprayed me in the eyes. They started to burn like someone set them on fire and tears were pouring out of my eyes even though they were squeezed so tight and I started walking backwards and I tripped on something and fell and felt pain at the back of my head and—you can guess what happened next— all went dark again.

I'm outside a grey house. The lawn looks abandoned. Empty cans of beer are sprouting where flower bushes are supposed to be. Grass is growing in between the cracks of the asphalt driveway. I walk to the door. It's dark red and something is oozing from the lock, something that resembles black tar. The handle is made of brass and it looks old. It has lost its shine and a green layer marks its age. I don't want to go in, but I must. Once inside, everything is dark, yet I'm able to see. A black couch sits in the middle. Black shelves and black curtains. I walk towards the kitchen. I'm thirsty. I turn the faucet and the water flowing is dark. I hold a glass under the stream of liquid. The water is dark red. I drink. I hear a voice calling from behind me and I turn. No one. I walk towards the door. The voice keeps calling me and it is distant and cold. A shiver runs down my spine. Every step I take is useless. I can move, but I'm always in the same place. I start running. I can't get anywhere. The ceiling starts moving. It's full of dark clouds coming down. I can't get anywhere. I keep trying hard to run. The voice keeps calling me. It's coming from the basement door. Now I can finally move properly and I'm standing in front of the door. I don't want to open the basement door. But I open it. There are stairs going down and the light returns to normal. The stairs are wooden and squeak with every step. I keep walking down and down, endlessly down. The walls are ruined with scratches. I try to speak, but my voice is silenced; I can't produce any sound. The stairs keep going down, endlessly down. I turn. I want to go back. The door is right behind me, but it won't open. I try to force the handle. Nothing happens. A laugh echoes on the other side of the door. A man's laugh. It scares me. I sit down. I want to cry.

The basement is dusty and full of things covered with blankets. In the middle there's a playhouse. It looks like the house I'm in. I look inside. In a room on the first floor two little girls are playing together with a small, stuffed, white rabbit. The same laugh comes from behind their door. The girls stop playing. They're scared. One runs and hides in the closet. The other stays there, still. The little door opens. A black figure, tall, enters the room. Everything is dizzy after it. Like the images are not ready to be shown yet.

seventeen

My eyes were still burning and I could keep the right one open only if I squinted it. I could feel Angelene's presence next to me. Her smell. The warmth of her body, like she was radiating heat. She said Sorry, and kept stroking my eyes with a damp cloth. It smelled like chamomile. Sorry, she said again. It's okay, I replied. After a couple of minutes I was able to keep my eyes semi-open again. They burned. I looked at Angelene. Her face looked soft and caring.

I didn't mean to hurt you, she said.

I know. I'm sorry. I should have known better.

You probably should have. But it's okay. I've seen the wound. Does it hurt?

Sometimes.

And my sister did that to you?

She did.

Angelene walked towards her purse that laid open on the chair and took out a pack of cigarettes and a lighter. She put one slim white cigarette in her mouth and lit it. Her left hand rested on her right elbow while her right hand held the cigarette. She took a deep breath in. The breath out was a long puff of whirling violet smoke.

She left me for dead, I said.

She took another puff. I said I'm sorry.

Maybe you can just help me find her. Then I'll be on my way.

She bit her lower lip.

Just help me find her and I'll go.

She took another puff, then said, I wouldn't know where to find her.

I stood up, slowly. My head was beating and spinning. I touched it on the back where it hurt the most and my hand was greeted by a big lump.

Ouch, I said.

You hit your head. You should see a doctor.

I'll be fine.

You were out for ten minutes, give or take. I was going to call an ambulance.

Was I?

Yes. But after the first five minutes I think you just fell asleep because you started moving. It was weird, though. You had bursts of movement and you were muttering things.

I think I had a bad dream, I replied.

It must have been really bad.

It was just unnerving. I kept stroking the back of my head, trying to recall the images. I was in what looked like an abandoned house, I told her, and I couldn't move. And I was locked in a basement and couldn't escape.

Angelene looked at me. A veil descended on her face. The skin around her eyes wrinkled and her mouth turned down.

Sorry. Why would you care.

Go on, tell me your dream.

Oh. Okay. Well, at least the basement wasn't dark. But I felt scared. I saw a small playhouse in the middle of it, and went closer.

Angelene walked towards her purse and took out another cigarette.

In the playhouse, on the first floor I could see two little girls playing with a stuffed toy. A small rabbit, I think. Then they heard a noise from outside. A laugh. And one of them hid and the other just stood there.

She brought the cigarette to her lips. Her hands were shaking. She managed to light it.

That's pretty much it. I just saw a tall black figure coming in from the door and then I woke up.

She took a long, deep breath. Smoke going out her nostrils.

Are you okay? You look upset, I said.

She didn't answer. Her eyes were lost somewhere other than this room. She held the cigarette with two fingers of her right hand while biting her right thumb. It was just a dream, I said, trying hard to understand why she looked so upset. She suddenly went to the bookshelf and grabbed the photograph frame. She looked at it. Her whole body trembled. I wanted to hug her.

Angelene? Are you alright?

She shook her head. Sorry, she said. Bad memories.

I stood up slowly and moved close to her. She didn't move. I put my hand on her shoulder and looked at the picture. It was the same picture I'd seen in Mallory's house, except this one was bigger—there was Mal's dad and Mal's mom and Mal, but the picture extended to reveal something more. Another girl who looked exactly like Mal. Angelene. The twins, together. They were smiling and the one that was cut out from Mal's picture was holding a stuffed toy.

A white rabbit.

She turned her body towards me and hid her face against my chest. I couldn't see her face, but I felt her tears and her body shaking and I hugged her. For reasons I can't explain, I felt tears in my own eyes. I fought them for a moment, but then gave up. I rested my face on her hair.

In the silence of the morning we stood there, two beings crying into each other; and Death was not around.

Angelene brewed two more cups of coffee. We rested our elbows on the kitchen counter. She poured out the coffee, and her story with it. Hers was not a happy family. Her mom Eliza was kindhearted and always joyful, a wild flower, a wild rose. And as often happens with fair souls who tread softly in this world, she ended up marrying her opposite. William. William, who was the head of the family and would provide food and shelter. William, who made all the decisions and took them to county fairs and to holiday houses on lakes.

William, who beat them and abused them.

Abuse and pain are things we try to push out of our minds, back onto a TV screen where we can pause and skip and feel safe while dreaming of the world that commercials sell. But there is no safety. Angelene smoked three cigarettes while she told me her story, and to this day I believe she kept the darker details from me. I was a stranger, but nonetheless she was opening herself up to me.

She lit the first cigarette when the story started to include more profound kinds of abuse. More physical ones. More degrading ones. The ones that turn a man into a monster and the lives around him into nightmares. You don't have to tell me that stuff, I said. She kept going. There's a point, she said. What usually happened was that William would come home very drunk. He'd strike one of the two girls at random. And they would pray he was drunk enough. Because drunkenness can be bliss when it ends with your nightmare asleep on the couch with white noise on the TV and the smell of hate and alcohol. But one night a police officer knocked on the door. He said that William probably didn't notice the sign for road works. And that some kids had probably stolen the sawhorses, so the road seemed clear. The police officer gently suggested they should sit down, Eliza and Angelene and her sister. The girls were now twenty-years-old, old enough to be called women. The officer kept his voice calm. He said that if only one of those mishaps didn't happen, William would have come back home and Eliza would have had to deal only with a drunk husband and not a dead one. But the officer didn't know the whole truth. And he went away leaving behind a chain of sorries, with not a doubt that the tears streaming down her face were tears of sorrow and desperation, not knowing that relief played a part.

Death can be a great ally, Angelene said, and I remembered that D was out there somewhere. She lit up the second cigarette and said,

But that isn't the point yet.

Oh.

The point is that it doesn't matter how much my dad hurt me and my sister. The point is that we missed him. And we hated each other because we missed him. Feelings have no written rules and they play strange games with your head. And we missed him night and day, but then, like the first rain after the summer, we also discovered the joy of a life without fear. And then, it started.

What started?

Mom. I don't know what got into her, but she started acting strange. At first they were just tarot readers. Then pretty quickly she started seeing self-proclaimed psychics. Mediums. Charlatans, if you want my opinion, she said while inhaling. It took very little for her to become obsessed. She wanted only one thing. She wanted to contact Dad. She was too frail to do this on her own. Too weak to live alone. She—Angelene paused and inhaled, arms crossed—justified Dad because her soul couldn't stand alone. She felt secure with him, even if he was who he was. She kept going to different people, the only result being that she was robbed of all her money. Our money. The smoke went out from her nostrils and her lips were worried and she kissed the cigarette again.

Eventually, she said, Mom got fed up. So instead of listening to people dressed up like third-rate magicians, she started buying books. She started studying and trying things herself. I suspect that in the beginning Mal helped her only to humor her. To be close to her. But she got dragged down into all that ancient bullshit. People need to believe. To hold on. The two of them would hole up for entire days studying all those dusty old books. I had to pick up two jobs just to keep us going while they tried to contact Dad. Or his ghost, if that makes sense.

It does, I said. Believe me.

Oh, so you're a believer? she asked.

Recent events have led me to change my mind on things I would've discounted as, let's say, bullshit.

Anyway. It was almost a year after Dad passed. I came back one night and found them.

Found them?

Mom and Mallory. They were in the kitchen, their hands red and dirty. It was gross. There was a headless animal corpse lying on the counter and blood sprays all over the walls and floor and weird signs engraved in wood panels. They were laughing and smiling at each other. Mal ran up to me and hugged me. He's back, she said. I asked What? and she said, Dad. Dad is back. Mom had her arms crossed, but wiped away a tear that was coming down her face, leaving a trail of blood on her cheek. They'd found a book, or more than one, and told me something about a ritual or a spell—something to bring the dead back. I thought they were crazy. They kept saying that they'd found a way to bring Dad back, and this is where it gets even weirder. They told me that they'd seen him. They saw him and his spirit, or his soul or whatever, could have still been here. Not for long, but enough to keep them looking for a better solution. They said they needed something to keep him here.

Like, attached to an object.

Precisely. How do you know that?

Your sister told me something similar.

She did, didn't she? I thought they'd gone crazy. I tried to calm them down and to reason with them, but it was useless. It was all too much for me. That was a Tuesday. Early on that Wednesday morning I left a note and was out of there. I caught the first ride out of the city and ended up here. She finished the second cigarette, stubbing it out in the ashtray.

I started making money the second day, would you believe it? I'd send some home and that was it. I wrote letters, but never got answers back. I tried calling, but as soon as they heard my voice they'd hang up. Then eventually the phone line was cut off. I didn't care. I didn't want to care. Does that make me a bad person? I don't care. I couldn't help them if they didn't want my help. That was three years ago. Six months ago I received a two-liner saying that Mom was sick and that I had to go home. So I did. It was the last time I saw either of them.

I'm sorry, I said.

I'm not. My mom was on her deathbed. Unable to speak. Or hear, for all I know. I never had the chance to say goodbye properly. And all that Mal could say is that we should have done something. That it was my fault. That if I'd stayed there Mom wouldn't have fallen ill. I was tired of only hearing accusations. We got into a fight. Mal shouted and said Mom stepped up her game before she got sick. She told me something, something I didn't want to hear or believe—Angelene paused to reach for the pack of cigarettes—It's crazy, she went on, as she took a cigarette out, put it in her mouth—but she told me that Mom found a spell. A powerful one. But there was something missing.

She lit up the third cigarette.

Human blood, and a body to use, is what Mal said to me.

Angelene paused, exhaling violet smoke out of her mouth.

eighteen

That final day Angelene started to believe that her sister was simply out of her mind. Angelene had never believed in ghosts or in an afterlife. And she knew her sister well enough to know that she wouldn't hurt another human being. But people change and put up shields around their real self, so Angelene told Mal to forget everything. Let go. And then they could be together again and everything would change for the better. But Mal had a different fire inside, and she insisted on going on with the spell. Angelene told her she was crazy. Together, we can do it, said Mal. Together. But Angelene stormed out of the house. Her sister was beyond help. I said,

So you left her alone, knowing that she planned on, basically, killing someone.

What would you have done? I didn't think she'd actually hurt anyone. She stopped trying to do crazy witch stuff after Mom got sick. She didn't have the heart to stab and kill animals all by herself, let alone do that to a human being.

I raised my shirt enough to show the patch over the stab wound. I guess you're right.

I'm sorry. I didn't stab you.

No, you didn't.

I could have stopped her then.

How?

I don't know. I could have helped her. I could have stayed.

I didn't speak.

Angelene didn't speak.

You should tell me where your old house is. I can check it out.

It's a four-hour drive, she replied.

I don't mind. My friend's with me.

Did he reply to your voicemail?

I pretended to check my phone quickly. No, I said.

Have you been friends for long?

Oh. I could say I've known *about* him all my life, but we just met recently.

I see.

Yep.

I noticed that she wasn't in her robe anymore. She must have changed while I was unconscious. She was wearing a black t-shirt and black jeans on black sneakers. I stared at her.

He'd love your style, I said, laughing. She looked down at herself.

What's wrong with it?

Nothing. He likes to dress in black, so I believe he'd approve.

It's just easier with basic colors. You don't have to waste time in the morning.

Plus, it's not like you need work clothes, I said.

She looked at me, narrowing her eyes and turning her lips down.

Sorry, I said, I didn't mean anything bad.

She didn't reply, but just kept staring at me.

I am truly sorry. I'm an asshole.

You kind of are, she said.

I felt a grip in my chest like someone was mauling my heart. I really apologize, I blurted out.

It's okay. People judge.

I kept quiet.

It's a job like any other. Better than others. I don't have to carry stuff around in a dirty truck or answer the phone every day for a company that sells toilet paper or be chained to a desk for a third of my life. I'm not selling my soul – or my body. I'm selling an image, a dream. Life is a dance on the edge of time and I do just that: I dance.

And you're pretty good at it, if I may say so.

Thanks, she said, and I couldn't help but notice the disbelief in her voice.

Where's the house, Angelene?

Angie. Wait here a moment, would you?

She moved quickly into another room. I waited, alone with the feeling of my idiotic failure, a failure that had wrecked any good impression I might have made on a fairy girl, one whose presence lightened my eyes and warmed my blood. I walked around the room, shuffling my feet nervously. The bookshelf. The books over there weren't about occult topics, as I'd feared. I recognized some of the names. Yeats. Thomas. Ginsberg. It was all poetry. Dickinson. I opened one: Spenser.

For of the soule the bodie forme doth take;
For the soule is forme, and doth the bodie make.

I closed the book when I heard her coming back. She had a small rucksack with her.

What's that for? I asked.

I'm coming with you.

What?

She let the bag drop onto the chair. What, is this a lone soul-searching journey?

Oh. Maybe. No. But I didn't see that coming. I paused and put my hands in my pockets. Are you sure? What about your job?

That's another one of the perks. I can take a couple days off.

That's, uh, good news.

Will your friend be okay with this? Is he coming?

I guess so. He'll have to. Be okay, I mean; I don't know if he'll come now.

And are you okay with that?

I think I have to be.

Good. We're set then.

Okay.

Okay.

There was a pause. Why are you doing this? I said.

Several reasons. Mainly because I feel like I have to help you, and I have to stop my sister before she hurts anyone else with her crazy ideas about ghosts and death.

Oh.

What's wrong?

Nothing. Just.

What?

Wait 'til we're on the road, then I'll tell you something crazy about ghosts and death.

Okay. If we don't need to wait for your friend, I think we should go. As I said, it's a long drive.

I believe he'll find us if needed.

We set out. The smell of the desert was dry and corrupt.

nineteen

Angelene looked at my old battered car and smiled. She caressed the lines of it like it was a pet. This small sign of affection for that old thing made me like her in a more profound way – the way that you discover once you've shaken off the attraction of the flesh, and bring in the empathy of the mind and heart and soul. In the bright light of the day and with my eyes still adjusting, I saw the girl under that beautiful skin, and I imagined her reading a poetry book, cup of coffee in one hand. I smiled, and we jumped in the car.

We slid over the dark asphalt, a mechanical boat on a concrete sea, while all around little dirt mountains and bushes made the landscape. Angie kept her thoughts to herself while the world outside went by. Sometimes people do crazy things like hopping in a car with a total stranger. We only hear those stories when they go rotten, but never the ones that end well because in this world good is not a story. I turned my eyes to look at the woman next to me, trying to see her again for the first time.

What? she said.

Nothing.

C'mon. What was it?

I was just thinking about the books at your place.

What about them? She adjusted herself on the seat so she could look at me more comfortably.

Nothing. I just didn't expect you to like poetry.

Because I'm an exotic dancer?, she said.

I could have smelled the hate in her words. No. No, not that, I said - Because all your sister had were books full of strange ideas.

I see.

But you'd agree that isn't a common thing?

Occult books?

No, the other one. A dancer that loves poetry.

Do you know many dancers?

I guess I don't. I kept looking at the road.

It isn't a common thing, she said. But not just for dancers. For people in general.

To love poetry? I said.

Yes. To love poetry.

I love poetry; I actually studied it.

Really? Who's your favorite author?

Let me think. Thomas. Dylan Thomas, I suppose.

Recite me one.

I wasn't used to reciting poems. I studied poetry because I wanted to understand the human soul. I didn't think it had any use, other than as a balm to keep evil away. I struggled to think of any poem. She smiled. Her eyes were jade that I wanted to steal. I opened my mouth to speak,

Dead men naked they shall be one
With the man in the wind and the west moon;

She looked at me, her eyes locked into mine, while the car rolled over the asphalt. And I let my soul in the hand of this lady, without looking at the road, unaware of reality again, and kept reciting the poem,

Though lovers be lost love shall not;
And death shall have no dominion.

There was no car, no time, no road. There was no faith, no evil, no sky. There was no sun, no sea, nothing else but the nakedness of the word, sliding from me to her and bouncing back from her eyes.

And Death shall have no dominion.

I finished the poem to the best of my memory. She had tears coming up the side of her eyes, which she wiped, unborn, before they came out. The phrase *You're very beautiful* scurried out of my mouth before I could stop it.

Thanks, she replied. She seemed genuinely pleased.

You *are* beautiful, I heard myself say, this time fully owning it. And your dance is a dance of pure beauty. I was mesmerized there.

She smiled faintly but genuinely, little wrinkles of an ancient soul grappling on the corner of her eyes, a confederacy of lines that people would call wrinkles but are just the fingerprints that life presses on you.

But I don' t understand, I said.

What?

Why? Why that place? I mean, I don't want to talk you out of your job. You're special when you do it, that's clear. Why that place though? Why not somewhere else?

I've worked in three different places since I've been living here, she said without losing her smile.

I nodded and turned my head again towards the road.

The first one was a simple club. Very plain and noisy. The girls were really nice to each other and the management was good with us. I made a lot of money with tips there, so I was happy. I stayed three months, the amount of time needed to learn the basics. Then a guy came in and told me he owned a big, swanky place, that I could make much more money in their VIP lounges and rooms. So I said okay and moved there.

She used her right foot to get rid of the left shoe and then used both hands to get rid of the right shoe. She took off her socks and stuffed them into one of the shoes. She then pushed the seat back a bit and raised her legs and rested her feet on the dashboard. From her new position she kept talking,

I had a private room in the place. A big clean room with a kitchenette and bath and view of the desert. I had people making my bed with fresh sheets every other morning. And yes, of course, money.

Why did you change? I asked.

Because. She paused. Can I smoke? she said while taking out her pack of cigarettes.

In the car? Do you have to?

I'll roll down the window, she said.

The desert air came in fast, dry, and hot. She lit a cigarette. Then kept talking,

So I changed because people in that place were filthy rich. Actually, they were just *filthy*. That was the kind of place with the sort of reputation that attracts the married guy on a business trip who wants *privacy*. The guy who's used to buying everything he wants and hates to be alone with himself. So these guys would come in and buy their dinner, their drinks, and their company for the night. Sometimes just for a dance or a talk. People are lonely. Everyone's lonely. - smoke drifted from her nostrils while she talked - and they're so used to having money, you know? They think they can buy something and not be lonely anymore, like I was a pill or something. But the worst part is that you're nothing more than an object to them. Something they can buy. And I'm not saying this against businessmen in general. There are good ones, of course, but I probably won't meet them. Anyway, you have no idea how many times I turned down money—a lot of money—and I looked like a freak because I didn't want to fuck these people. All the fucking time.

She noticed that the car was getting smoky and rolled the window down a bit more to change the air, then she smashed the cigarette in the ashtray and closed the window back up. The air conditioner chugged behind the dashboard, helping us regain a non-melting temperature.

I suppose that's a normal thing in your line of work, I said.

It is, but you can do it in many different ways. You see, I left home with no plans, but I still wanted to help people. I still wanted to do something with my life. In a place like that, the only thing I could have done was sell myself out.

I glanced at her. I don't mean to offend, but I don't see how things have changed for the better.

Ugh, I have to explain everything to you, don't I? She adjusted her position on the seat and loosened the belt. Then said, Every one of us is looking for only one thing.

Sex? .

Sex is part of it, yes, she replied. What is sex? A biological mechanism. Humans and only a very few animals have sex not just for biological reasons. But I believe that it's even more profound for us. We have sex because we want to connect with someone. The most precious thing in the world is when you feel *connected*; it makes you feel alive. It makes you feel like you exist, she said, while gently thumping her right fist twice on the middle of her chest.

I nodded.

So in a place like the one I was in, people were just used to buying things. But the real thing they were trying to buy was this human connection they craved so badly. But that's beyond their reach. They buy it and the next day they forget about it. They push the emptiness that they have inside deep down in their throats and their hearts, which will eventually fail.

That phrase reminded me of Neil. I swallowed and kept looking at the road.

They go back to their wives, girlfriends. They go back to their empty apartments with a false feeling of success. But they just bought a cheap knockoff of the real one, and as soon as they realize it, they look for it again.

She went to take another cigarette from the pack but stopped. She looked out of the window.

I looked at her, then at the road again. She continued,

So I changed place. The place where you found me doesn't offer fresh beds and champagne, and the people who try to buy me are offering much less than the other place, but it doesn't matter because I'm not selling. In a place like the one you found me you'll rarely see rich people. Customers there aren't the same as everywhere else. They're not the young, not the rich, not the tourists. The people in there are the desperate ones who try so hard not to wear their heart on their sleeve that their faces become cages for their fears. People in there are looking to be on the edge just enough to hide what they believe is their ugliness. It might be a deformed face or a fat body, a small cock jeered at too many times during gym class. It doesn't matter. What matters is that they're alone and always have been and they're scared that this is how it's gonna end: *alone*. So they go to a place where they're among people like themselves. They go amongst the losers. They go to a place where they think they can hide, where they can find a cure. A balm for their aches. Other humans who look at them without judgment because they're in the same gutter.

She took the cigarette out of the pack and toyed with it, rolling it up and down her fingers, and continued,

But in that orgy of lights and shadows and sweat and dollars you can catch a glimpse of their face for a second, and look them in the eye; and if you're in that place you're like them, and that split moment when your eyes meet the only thing that goes on in between is nothing but three simple words: *I see you.* I don't look at them to give them false promises and hopes of sweat and bodies clamped together in some naked primordial dance. I look at them and I tell them with my eyes, *I see you.*

She turned her body completely towards me and stared. I felt the need to look at her. Into her eyes, while she said,

I see *you.*

And lit up the cigarette.

twenty

The road was now running fast under our wheels. The silence that fell in the car matched the emptiness of the desert around us. But suddenly, as the road turned bigger, there were too many cars and too much traffic and human beings at junctions and you could go crazy trying to figure out every single universe that every single being was carrying around in their mind; locked in thoughts and running around.

What really happened with my sister? Angelene said, breaking the silence.

What do you mean? I told you the story.

It's not the truth, though, is it?

I sighed, then said, If I tell you the truth you'll think I'm crazy.

Believe me, I already think so.

Yet you're in a car with me.

That's to find my cuckoo sister.

You have a thing for crazies.

Her eyes held a genuine smile and she shook her head. C'mon. What happened?

It's a long story.

Are you going someplace outside of this car in the next few hours?

Huh. No, not really.

So shoot.

Alright.

This time I told the whole story as I'd experienced it. The only thing I left out was the fact that I'd passed the night with her sister, but I was sincere about everything else, like a kid who knows he's been caught and the only recourse he has is to confess.

I told her how Neil died. I told her about my faded memories and weird dreams. I told her that her sister could see Neil. I told her that I could see Neil, but only when I was drunk. On tequila.

Any specific brand of tequila? she asked sarcastically.

Very funny. I think any brand works.

Then I took a deep breath and felt like I was gambling my whole credibility on a single phrase. I told her that the three of us—Neil, Mal, and me—believed that on that given night we'd had an encounter with the personification of Death. I looked at her to see her reaction. Her face didn't show any feeling at all. I said it again.

We met the Grim Reaper.

She burst out laughing. It's not funny, I said. She kept laughing. Small drops of tears were gathering at the edges of her eyes and she intercepted them with the edge of her wrist. I'm sorry, she said, in between laughs. When she eventually calmed down enough to be able to contain her amusement, she said,

I'm sorry, really. It's just absurd. Crazy.

You wanted the truth.

I know. I am sorry.

She stabbed me, you know.

Yes, I know that - she became immediately serious, then added, Sorry.

Okay.

Why did she stab you then, exactly?

To contact Death again, I guess. That's what she told me. To perform a ritual.

And then what?

That was my question to her. But she looked like she knew what she was doing.

I think she tricked you.

That looks clear to me, I replied.

I mean, she was definitely using you for some of her crazy rituals. She just played with your sorrow for the loss of your friend. She said she could see your friend, right?

Yes.

And was it true? Did she see him? Or speak to him?

I squinted my eyes, trying to recall. Actually, no, I said. She never talked with him. Or vice versa for that matter. Not that I noticed.

She had a grin on her face that to me meant, sorry, buster, but you fell for it. But she kept silent.

She described him to me! I shouted. How could she possibly know?

Well, I don't know. Did you have a picture of him with you? Anything she could have seen?

No.

Did you tell her his name and your name? She could have looked at you, and him, on the Internet. That's an easy thing to do.

I don't think she knows my surname. Or Neil's.

When did she describe him to you? Angie asked.

It was the day after the fun - the *funeral*! It was in the small cemetery in the town and there was a big picture of Neil. I left Mal's place and went to the funeral. She was out already. She could've followed me and sneaked in and — oh my god, I am stupid, stupid! I banged my hand on the wheel in bursts of anger.

Angie put her hand on my shoulder and then stroked my right cheek, and said,

Don't be. You were in pain. She used it.

Fuck her. Fuck her!

That, you wanted to do, apparently.

What does that even mean?

Oh, come on. It's a fucking play, don't you see? She used your sorrow and your all-male need to put your *thing* everywhere you can. It's Woman-Tricks-Man 101. Don't get mad. That's how the world has always been. This'll make you smarter, she said, and then added in a soft voice, almost impossible to hear, And *I'm* the family slut.

I took deep breaths. Focused on the road. I can't wait to find her, I said, tightening my grip on the wheel.

We'll find her. We will. Angie stroked my cheek with the outside of her hand again, and smiled at me.

But it's not over, I said.

No, it's not.

My story I mean.

Oh. Sorry. Then go on.

Here comes the best part.

Okay. I'm ready.

Something happened after she stabbed me.

This time she didn't laugh but said, Explain, please.

When your crazy bitch sister stabbed my gut, something actually happened. I was bleeding out. She was there chanting and doing her crazy stuff. Neil got crazy and started hovering around her. Then the colors changed. Everything went, like, frozen. Time stopped. Everything was slow. I started shivering. Then he came.

He?

Yes. He. The whatever you want to call it. Death.

She swallowed.

He came and we talked.

You talked?

Yes. And played chess.

Now she looked worried.

I won, I said, smiling.

She shifted in the seat. You saw Death and played chess with him. And won.

Yes.

Does that make you immortal? she said.

Oh, no. It doesn't work like that. It was just a game; he does it to pass the time.

He does what?

Death. He wanted to pass the time, so we played.

Angie's look became more and more worried. You're telling me that not only did you see your friend's ghost, which would be crazy enough, but that you actually *believe* you met Death and played chess with it.

Yes.

Okay. That's it. I don't know who's crazier, you or my sister.

Oh, it doesn't stop here.

What? she said, turning quickly towards me. What now? Is Death here with us? Your dead friend? What else?

No, he's not here now. But you remember I spoke of a friend that was with me, don't you?

Her eyes widened.

So, that friend was him. Death. The Grim Reaper.

She looked at me with a worried eye.

He stayed with me in the hospital, and drove with me to find you. Then just outside your house, he disappeared. But I have the feeling he's not gone. Maybe he just didn't want to scare you. I don't really know.

She took the pack of cigarettes out of her purse and crushed it when she realized it was empty.

I need a smoke, she said. Can you stop somewhere?

Sure. Soon as we find a place that sells tobacco.

Thanks.

I'm not crazy, I said.

Well, you're definitely not normal.

I didn't stab anyone.

I didn't either. So if there's one person in this car who has the right to be upset and scared, well that's fucking me.

She crossed her arms and stared out at the road. The road was silent, an unaware path of all the worlds that ran upon it.

At the gas station Angie lit up a cigarette near the car. I came closer.

Give me one, I said.

What?

Give me a cigarette.

Have you ever smoked?

In high school. Because it was *cool*.

Why'd you stop?

Because it wasn't that cool. She offered me the lighter and I offered the tip of my cigarette. I coughed a little when the smoke hit my lungs. She giggled.

It's been a long time, I said.

It's okay. You're right. It's not the healthiest habit, but hey, you gotta die someday.

Yeah.

She took a deep breath and while exhaling asked, Did he tell you?

What? I asked.

How you die. When.

Are you talking about, about, I said, hanging on the last word.

I'm talking about Death. You're pals, right?

We are.

Then did you ask him?

I did not.

She groaned. You hang out with Death and you don't ask him when you're gonna die.

It didn't seem like he knew, I said, and took another puff.

Can I ask him if we meet him?

About me?

No, silly. About me.

Sure, but I doubt he knows. He's my Death.

What do you mean by that?

It's complicated. He said everyone has their own Death. You'd have to ask yours.

Well, I think I'll do that, but I have a feeling I'll know the same time she does.

She?

Angie took another drag on her cigarette and said, If everyone has their own Death, why can't mine be a she? I don't like the idea of a man being the one who accompanies me wherever it is that I'll have to go.

I see. So, are you starting to believe me now?

She gripped the cigarette in her thumb and middle finger, then launched it in a wide arc. It ended up in a small pool of water from the building's air conditioning unit and fizzled out. She looked at me and said,

No, I don't believe you, she said. I believe you dreamed it all, or that you're a schizophrenic or something.

Thank you, I said sarcastically.

Don't get me wrong. I don't think you're dangerous. To me at least. And I also think that people experience stuff that I have no clue about. And even if it's not real, well, the experience is. You might not have seen your dead friend, or Death. *Your* Death. But the experience you had, true or not, doesn't change what you felt, does it?

I nodded. Then shook my head. Then nodded again.

So I don't really care. And I delayed confronting my sister for too long. I thought I could simply leave it behind, but look at me. She looked around, with her hands in the back pockets of her jeans. I was doing well, and you knocked on my door. With news about my sister. If that's not fate at work, I don't know what else it could be.

So you don't believe me.

Sorry, Louis.

It's alright. I just wonder where D is.

D?

Death.

Oh. Right, you're friends.

Stop it, would you? I said, and fist-bumped her shoulder lightly. She smiled.

Tell me what your Death looks like?

Okay, once we're on the road again.

She sat down in the passenger seat. And I'll tell you how I'd like mine to look, she said, while closing the door.

I imagine she'll be incredibly beautiful. Like you, I said to the air like the coward I am, unsure if I hoped the car wasn't soundproof enough to keep my words outside, or vice versa.

I got into the car and smiled at Angie. She smiled back.

Maybe I did dream it all, I thought. Maybe there are no ghosts and what we think is an immortal soul, a stream of consciousness, is indeed just the way we perceive ourselves. The continuity of our experience is what shapes our self. We perceive and create our own world bit by bit. In the end, we are self-perceiving universes of our own, lost in a sea of other universes that clash and fight and fall in love. The only moments when we are truly alone are when we are the only human being born and the only one who's dying, but all in between we are one and many altogether, trying to make sense of time.

twenty-one

The road trip continued on a lighter note. We talked about poetry, about life, and to an external eye, we might have looked like two lovers on their first vacation. We laughed, and the old interior of the car became our little piece of world for a while. Then the landscape opened out onto two big mountains with white caps of snow. They seemed out of place after all the road in the red desert. The sun was already on the other side of the world and the street we took was without streetlights. We drove north for a couple of miles; all around us was darkness and the shapes of trees. Eventually she told me It's here and I pulled over and into a white pebble driveway.

The house from my dream.

Clearly abandoned for at least a couple of years. The lawn was just weeds. No cans of beer. I parked and looked at Angie. Her eyes caught mine and she smiled uncomfortably. I touched her face with my hand and told her, It'll be okay, I don't think anyone's here.

We got out of the car. The door wasn't red and no black plasma was seeping through it. So far, so good. Angie shook her purse and put her hand in, fishing out a set of keys. She walked up to the door and inserted the key, then took a deep breath. The lock clicked; we were in.

In a living room. On the left were a small desk, a mirror, and some forgotten jackets. Two worn-out couches stood in the middle. No signs of anyone living there. Dark. The air smelled like an empty water bottle left closed in the sun for too long. Dust covered everything. I could see the arch opening to the kitchen. Angie tried the switch, but nothing happened, so I said,

It's the main.

I'll go outside, she said.

I'm coming with you, I replied.

For as much as it seemed that I didn't want to leave her alone, it was the complete opposite. The sheer normality of the house gave me chills. How everything settled, just waiting to disappear. A *clank* of the main was followed by a faint humming sound.

Light.

I could see on Angie's face the weight of the memories coming back. She wandered around the room looking at everything and nothing, stopping at a wall with family pictures on it. She stayed there, arms crossed. I looked around and could figure out a door that was probably the basement door, and a staircase to the upper floor. I said nothing, leaving Angie space and time to cope with her thoughts. With her past. After a couple of minutes she said,

There's no one here. And it doesn't look like anyone's been here. For a long time.

I agree, I said, and ran my finger along the coffee table. I showed my grey fingertip to Angie.

Not that we had a plan anyway, she said.

I believe you might talk some sense into her.

I don't.

What do we do now?

I felt like we were getting nowhere. I put my hand in my pocket and reached for Neil's watch. I took it out and looked at it. Looked around. Nothing. Angie sat on the couch and sighed,

We have to see exactly what Mal is planning to do. We have to find a clue. Anything.

I agree.

Last time I was here, there were books everywhere. Now it's tidy. It's like nothing happened.

I looked around. Mal had some books in her house, I said. But not as many as it sounds like you saw.

Then she must have left some of them there. And there were notebooks from my mom.

Mal had a notebook. Just one. A big one.

There were many, Angie said.

So we find those things. We try to understand what's going on in her mind.

And if she's gone cuckoo, we call the police. Like you should have done.

I nodded. Where do you think all the books could be?

Angie turned her head towards one of the doors. The basement, she said.

I looked at the door. Walked to it. Opened it. An ancient smell of rot. A smell of death coming swiftly up from the staircase that ran down into the darkness. With just a faint light coming from behind me I could imagine the scratches on the side of the walls. From small animals.

Or small people.

I didn't go down straight away, like a child scared of the dark. I closed the door and turned to Angie. She stood up from the couch.

Maybe they're upstairs, I said. The books, I mean.

She shook her head. Upstairs is just bedrooms and bathrooms. Besides, I don't want to go there.

Her face twisted and she wrapped her arms around herself. She gave another uncomfortable smile, her eyes fixed on the stairs. I had the feeling that whatever bad thing had happened to her happened upstairs. She looked at me and said, We have to go down.

I nodded and opened the basement door again. This time I flicked the switch and the light showed the end of the staircase. A normal staircase to a normal basement. Angie followed me down. Heaps covered with blankets, probably furniture. Old bikes. Two big tires. The old heating furnace at the far end, and in the middle, a dark wood table, and on top of it, a pile of books and notebooks.

We found them, I said.

We started to check the books. All of them were about occult practices and ancient rituals and spells. There were mythological books, religious books, pagan books. There was no clear sign of a pattern, no sign of someone trying to make up their mind about what's next – the whole looked like a desperate attempt, the kind of attempt you try when you lose any hope.

Some of the books had highlighted passages. Some had notes scribbled on the margins, dates, but nothing of immediate importance. The craziness of it all was a mirror of the minds that set everything in motion. With all the happenings of the last days, I found myself shocked to learn that this was the first time I actually felt lucky enough to be alive. After having met Mallory.

We realized that the books were not the key to Mal's intentions, and diverted our focus to the notebooks. We gathered up the pile of them, carrying it upstairs. I was glad to get out of there.

The notebooks were indeed more interesting. Carefully filed with every year, month, and day, they told the story of Angelene and Mallory's mom. The first one started as a diary. Of things that weren't going as planned. The story that Angelene told me was retold word by word in the first notebook. The second started with confessions of relief. Of hope. But the hope was suddenly transformed into fear. The scribbling became less and less clear and Angie had to slow down to figure out what was written.

It was a story of madness. It spoke of strange dreams that started haunting Angie's mom, Eliza. William was calling her from somewhere, but she couldn't see him or touch him. Eventually she was able to talk to him in a dream and he told her beautiful things. That if he had the chance to come back, everything would be different.

She believed it, I said.

She did, Angie closed the notebook. Aren't you having weird dreams like that?

What are you saying?

Nothing. Just that it's normal to dream of people you love when they're dead.

Not when you see them in real life.

You were drunk. You said so.

I was. But that's not why I saw Neil.

Or Death.

Or him, for all I know.

Better keep reading, she suggested.

The end of the second notebook was just pages and pages of dreams. About William, the father and husband. The man in the dreams was a caring and loving one. Eliza dreamed of her husband for six months before telling her daughters. She truly believed that death had changed her husband and, more importantly, that he wasn't out of reach. That's when she started studying, to learn how to communicate with a world that has never spoken back.

The third notebook's handwriting was calmer, heavier on the page. It showed resolution and clarity. Focus. The same kind of focus geniuses have. We read about the failed attempts with candles and chants. With small animals. Old Latin spells mixed up with Caribbean voodoo and African juju. Demonic invocations and walks in the moonlight to dig stuff at crossroads. All sorts of beliefs were mixed up in a desperate attempt to make something work. To make sense of things we don't want to accept.

All the Gods that humanity created, all the Demons, all of them received a prayer from Eliza.

The house was silent and I could hear the small crackling of Angie's cigarette and her breath in and out while we read the same pages with our bodies close on the couch.

The fourth notebook started with a revelation. Something worked. Something made of pagan formulas and voodoo killing rituals involving blood. Eliza and Mal were ecstatic about the result, but Angie didn't understand. The story of how Angelene decided to leave home was told by different eyes here. A mother's eyes. A mother who felt betrayed and abandoned in a moment of need. A mother that felt her child didn't want her father back. But also a mother who worried about her little girl and couldn't wait for the day to be reunited with her.

Angelene was crying. I didn't notice immediately. She didn't make any sound and her body didn't move. But you can't stop the soul ebbing from the eyes, and all I could do was put my arm around her shoulder, kiss her on the forehead, and stay put and silent. Because sometimes plain existing is the only thing you remember how to do. I put my other arm around her, and in some kind of osmosis I felt a wave of sorrow unleashing itself and possessing me, and there, in a strange house with a stranger in my arms, I cried all the losses of my life.

After our tears dried we didn't talk for some minutes. We looked around and went back to the basement that had lost its aura of evil - because evil is in the eyes of the beholder. We looked everywhere, and hand in hand our hearts gave courage to each other. Angelene sighed, but decided to go with me upstairs where I discovered the rooms of two young girls and a bathroom and another bedroom, the main one. We looked under the beds and in the closets. We looked behind the curtains and behind the pictures and knocked on the floors. Nothing. Angelene didn't want to be left alone in any of the rooms and she kept looking behind herself. Jumpy as a cat. She kept close to me and hugged my arm, following me like a shadow.

The fifth notebook was missing.

The heart of the night was approaching fast. Our bodies were tired. Our spirits were tired. We were lazily shuffling through pages and rereading notebooks in no particular order. We didn't find any clue as to where Mal could be. She was simply gone.

I'm starving, Angelene said.

Now that you mention it, me too.

We could go into town and eat something.

I think that's a very good idea.

We didn't move.

Do you often have weird dreams, Louis? Angie asked.

Normal frequency, I'd say.

Do you know what lucid dreaming is?

I think I heard about it.

It's when you know you're dreaming.

I usually wake up when I realize it's a dream.

Angie crossed her legs on the couch. They say that if you become aware of yourself in your sleep, you can do anything you want.

Sounds fun, I replied, distractedly.

It can be. But it comes from an ancient practice.

Of course it does.

Really. Monks used to say that if you master your dream self, then you'll be able to master Death itself. To be present and aware when your consciousness moves on. You could extend the final moment and make it last forever.

How do you know all of this? I asked.

Everyone deals with grief in her own way. I dealt with it by trying to understand what happens when we die.

And? Do you have an answer?

Angie laughed. No, I don't have one. *You* are the friend of the Grim Reaper, she said, smiling at me.

I sighed. Good. We're back to mocking me.

I'm sorry, but it's just not very believable.

I know. Good friend he is, disappearing like that and making me look like a crazy man.

Didn't you say you only see him when drunk?

No, that's my otherworldly ghost-friend Neil. And it's not when I'm drunk; being drunk is the side effect. I think even just tipsy works. But it has to be tequila. I instinctively put my hand on my pocket to feel the shape of the watch. Angelene stood up. It seemed like she'd just remembered something. She smiled at me softly and went over to a small cabinet, turned the key and opened it. There were half-empty bottles of decade-old alcohol.

Mom used to put water in all the bottles, she said. To make them lighter when Dad would drink them. We couldn't get rid of the alcohol; he'd get angry, she said while emptying the cabinet. But he hated tequila. It made him gag. Where is it? Ah! Found it!

She turned around. In her hands a bottle of tequila, unopened.

What? I asked.

What, you say? That's tequila. It was a gift from someone I don't even remember. Dad never opened it. Looking back, maybe we could have saved him by simply mixing tequila into all the other bottles. She went into the kitchen and materialized with two glasses.

I don't think that's a good idea, I said.

You said you can see stuff when you're tipsy, right? Let's verify your theory.

Last time I drank with one of the Day girls, I ended up half-dead in a hospital.

Let's not make comparisons here. It's just to wind down. We've had a long day. She poured two glasses. Then we go eat. Deal?

I took one of the glasses. Smelled it. The alcohol hit my nose immediately, made stronger by years in the same bottle.

See, I think alcohol and drugs are good things.

Of course you do, I said.

Don't judge. Alcohol and drugs can open doors you never even thought were there. They bring visions.

I kept smelling the alcohol from my glass.

But those visions from chemicals aren't there for us to take. She raised the glass to me. Real visions only come in silence and meditation.

I clinked my glass against hers and we both drank.

I'm taking a leap of faith here, Louis. Let's say I believe you. Let's say you do have a gift; you can see things we humans are not supposed to see.

I think I would have noticed if I had a gift like that, I said.

Really? No weird kid stories? Don't you have memories of strange things happening and adults telling you that it was just a bad dream?

I believe we all have, I said, and took another sip. The alcohol was evaporating and the taste of tequila was, for once, a warm and familiar one.

And what if those bad dreams weren't dreams? What if in dreams we walk worlds we're not supposed to walk? She knocked back the glass in one shot and poured herself another.

That wouldn't change anything about the waking world, I said.

It does for me.

And why's that?

All men whilst they are awake are in one common world: but each of them, when he is asleep, is in a world of his own, Angelene said.

I widened my eyes at her.

That's old. From some Latin poet.

It means that what happens in dreams is yours and yours only.

I finished my tequila and poured a second one, filling the tumbler to its top. I could feel the alcohol already working in my blood.

You should know your poets, mister, she said.

I smiled and said, I do know them. I might not remember them, but their words stay with me long after I've read a poem. Maybe I'm not good at recalling them line by line, but I do feel them. All the time.

I see, she said.

She hid her mouth in the glass. She took another sip. Her cheeks started to get a bit of color from the drink. Her lips were red and she smiled at me, then said,

I'm sorry. I'm emotional about all this. It's woken up some memories. She lit a cigarette.

I sipped another bit of tequila, looked around the room, scanning for a sign.

Anything? She asked.

What? Oh. No. There's no one around, I said, looking at the room.

She nodded. I put my hand in my pocket and brought out Neil's watch. I put it on the table in front of us.

What's that? Angie asked.

It's a pocket watch.

I can see that.

It belonged to Neil.

I see.

It belonged to Neil, and your sister told me to hold on to something of his to help him stay here. Like a lighthouse to find his way. So I kept it.

I took a good swig of tequila and looked around. The air was as empty as my heart. She moved closer to me. In the dim light of the only lamp we left on, her eyes were shimmering emeralds. I sighed and fought the tears.

I miss Neil. And he's gone forever, I said.

Angie started caressing my cheek with the outside of her hand. Then she opened it and put the other one on my other cheek so my face was held by her palms. She moved even closer and looked me in the eyes and then she kissed my forehead and looked back into my eyes. Smiled at me. I moved my face towards hers and was about to kiss her. Maybe drinking tequila on an empty stomach didn't help, but whatever got into me made me lose my balance and to stop myself from toppling forward I ended up with my hands on her hips and my face in her breasts. She shoved me away and jumped up.

Fuck you! she shouted.

God, I'm sorry; I lost my balance!

Lost your balance. You're a pervert. You're a fucking pervert.

No, I swear I'm sorry! Angie! I shouted.

She ran for the door, and I jumped up and followed her outside. The air was slimy and cold. Would you stop? I asked.

She turned. What?

I'm sorry, I said.

Sorry, my ass.

Listen. I wanted to kiss you, that is true. But I lost my balance! It's the goddamn alcohol!

It's always the alcohol, right? She crossed her arms.

I am sorry.

She kept silent.

I didn't mean to hurt you.

She sighed and said, I know. I'm sorry.

I walked slowly towards her.

I—it's the house. It has terrible memories.

I understand, I said, and reached my hand towards her.

Don't touch me, she said, while jumping back and flinging her arms up.

I won't.

I think we should go, she said. Her face was pale. She kept looking at me, then the house, and back at me again.

Where? I asked.

Anywhere. I'm not sleeping there, she said, pointing at the house.

We'll find a motel, I said.

Good. And tomorrow morning we'll go to the police. So you can end this story and go back to your life. And I'll go back to mine.

Okay. It only makes sense, I said.

Let's go.

I think I forgot the watch. I'll go get it.

Do as you wish.

You're not coming in? You'll get cold.

No way I'm going in there now.

I looked at the door of the house that had closed itself. Then I looked at Angie, scared in the dark and alone. It was just a watch. Neil was dead anyway.

I don't need it now, I said, and moved towards the car.

On the way back to the city we didn't talk, and Angie just looked out the window. Whatever had happened in that house had stayed under her skin all those years. We found a motel open twenty-four hours, checked into two separate rooms, waved goodnight with the promise to end this trip the next day, with the hanging menace of not seeing each other again. That was probably my last night with the woman I fell for, and we were spending it like two strangers, at arm's reach but worlds apart. We were jaded, and it wasn't for the miles we had under our feet but for the cracks that the road had opened in our minds. I closed the door behind me. I sat on the bed and turned on the TV. White noise. I turned the TV off and went out and walked to a liquor store. Almost on autopilot, I bought a small bottle of tequila, walked back to my room, and opened the bottle.

Smell of freshly brewed coffee. I look around. Angie's there, in underwear and one of my t-shirts. Her hair is tied up in a loose bun. She is lit by the early morning sun. She must have slept here. I get out of bed and walk through the bedroom door into the living room. The sun is low and new, slicing light in through the half-opened blinds. I sit down at the table and Angie walks towards me. Silently kisses my forehead. I had a bad dream I say, and she doesn't reply. She carries over the coffee pot and pours some in my cup. Small bubbles frothing on the side like little black pearls. I sip the coffee and take out my phone to call Neil. The other side rings in my ear, once and then twice. Someone picks up.

What's up?

Neil?

No. It's my sister.

Neil.

Louis, are you okay?

I don't know, Neil. You were dead.

What now?

I had a dream and in it you were dead.

Was I? Huh.

You were. And someone did something bad to me. Something bad. You saw it and tried to stop it, but then disappeared and I felt like I lost you forever.

That sounds like me, Neil said.

Where are you?
I'm at the house.
The house.
You were there yesterday.

I sip once more from the cup, now an empty glass of tequila. I look around and wave at the bartender. One more. Neil is next to me having a beer. He is well-dressed. On the far side of the bar there is a girl pole dancing. I want to check that it isn't Angie, but I don't move as the bartender brings me another glass of tequila.

How's Death? says Neil.
Sorry?
Death. The Reaper.
Oh. He's okay I guess. How's yours?
Mine as well. Mine as well. He drinks half of his beer.

I drink half my tequila. You're bleeding, Neil says, and picks up two toothpicks. With the toothpicks he stabs me right in the heart. Blood starts to flow and it stings in the center of my chest. He lays a napkin on the toothpicks to stop the bleeding. It doesn't work.

The ceiling is moving and I see a thousand birdcages with small black birds in them. They look like little crows. All the girls in the bar start undressing and dancing. I keep looking for Angie but she isn't there. The cages open with a metallic sound and the birds fly, covering the air with black spots. Go to the house, Louis, says Neil, and disappears in a mist of dark wings.

I'm now someplace that looks like a courthouse. I am in the stand. The jury is composed of mannequins; they all resemble me, at different ages. There is Louis as a boy and Louis as a young man and Louis as an old man. And Louis as I am now. The judge enters slowly and I recognize it immediately. It's the giant crow I saw the night Neil died. I'm not afraid. All the birds gather around me.

A parliament of crows.

One of them, the bigger, starts talking, with its cawing morphed into human words,

Dear mate, you are gathered here today in front of this jury, he says with a rasping voice that doesn't come from his beak. Then continues, Oh, who am I kidding? Let's cut the crap.

He opens one of his wings and Neil is under it. Then he opens the other and a beautiful woman is there, her hair red like the shade of the sun when it's dead and her lips blossoming like roses. She has green eyes and pale skin. Her belly is naked and I can see it growing bigger and bigger before my eyes; she is pregnant. She spreads her legs and from the bottom of her dress two little girls emerge painlessly. Mallory and Angelene. The woman's dress is quickly shifting to a darker shade, fluid. Like blood. I look around and the two girls are now adults and naked, and even if their bodies share a striking resemblance, they do not share the same beauty.

Under the bird's wings are Neil, Mallory, and Angelene. All of them naked. We're under the stars, in what looks like an ancient Roman arena. The moon is shining and the clouds are broken and remade by the wind in an endless dance.

Who are you gonna save? the bird declares.

All of them, I reply.

No, you won't, because you cannot save anyone but you.

The bird flaps his wings once, twice. The air coming from them throws me to the ground. Angelene and Mallory and Neil turn into skeletons and their bones shine like constellations.

When I manage to stand up I'm alone in a large field. Far away I see the voluptuous red-haired woman, hand in hand with Mallory and Angelene, going away. I shout but no sound comes from my throat. I want to move but I am not able to. I turn around. Neil is there. He's talking; his mouth moves but I can't hear any sound. I want to talk to him but can't make my voice go out of my throat. He moves towards me slowly, and with every step he is more out of focus. When he gets close he's just a blurred spot of color. I reach out to touch him. Warmth and sadness. Then a pop! echoes in the air, like a bubble bursting, and sounds are coming in again. Neil is standing next to me. I'm in a parking lot and my car is not there and there is only an old motorbike. Neil goes to the bike and turns a lever on the side of it and turns it on. Then he signals for me to go with him. We ride on tree-covered roads until we reach a small, white house on the side of a lane. I recognize it as Angelene's house. It looks much newer. In the garden are two little girls playing. When I step off the bike Neil is no longer there. I look around and the garden is empty. With every step I take, the color of the house darkens. When I get to the door the building is black and the door red. I put my hand on the handle.

We meet again, a familiar voice behind me says. I turn. In his skinny jeans and sneakers, Death himself.

Hi, I say.

Hi.

Where have you been?

Where I always am.

I didn't see you.

He smiles gently. Love can do that, he says. It makes me disappear.

What's going to happen here, D?

You know what is going to happen, my boy.

I don't.

Then you will remember.

I've never been in there. Not like this, I say.

You have been, but you have not experienced it yet.

I understand.

Do you?

This time I think I do. Will you be there as well?

I am always there. I am there at night while you forget and I am there again when you remember.

You know what I mean.

No.

Will I meet you there?

You have already met me. You have not experienced me.

Will I?

Everyone will, in their own time, in their own way.

And what will happen then?

The same thing that happens when you love and when you dream.

I smile at him. He smiles back and nods. Go, he says.

I turn the handle and go in. There I see the beautiful red-haired woman. Her skin is porcelain and her eyes are soft and warm and maternal. She's on a couch, with Mallory and Angelene in her arms, asleep. She smiles at me. I move closer. The girls are still naked. I reach out and touch Angelene. I swiftly retract my hand. She's cold. Their skin is grey and there is no shine in their eyes.

Dead. Both of them.

twenty-two

With a jerk I sit upright on the bed. Covered in cold sweat, I find myself panting.

Another dream. Another nightmare. Another play behind the scenes.

And although I couldn't recall what made me run out of my sleep, my skin was prickling with an ominous sensation. I felt like the world was about to crumble and there was nothing I could do to stop it. My head was spinning from the tequila. I looked at the bottle. Empty. I didn't remember when I stopped drinking, but I was sure I didn't drink all of it.

I moved my hand on the bed sheets to check if some of it spilled over, but they were dry, proof of my insanity, proof of me drinking the night away. I passed my hands through my hair and over my face. Rough skin met my palms. It had been days without a shave. My heart still didn't believe it was back in real life. With a tingling feeling in my chest, I moved to the bathroom.

Ten minutes later I was out, showered, teeth brushed, mouth swilled. Ten to eight, said the clock on the wall. Angelene might still be sleeping. I needed to get rid of that dreadful feeling. And of my headache. Lately, that was the only thing that tequila brought me—

no more magic visions, no more touching the unknown, no more life after death; the only visions I got from it were lost in a haze of memories and fake dreams, and all that left behind was destruction in my head.

I looked on the desk for the car keys. Instead, I saw a rectangular piece of white paper with a scribble on it. I took it. It was Angie's writing.

Sorry about yesterday. I woke up early. You didn't lock your door. I'm at the house getting your watch. Objects have meaning. See you when you're awake.

- Angie

At the house. I wasn't able to appreciate the apologies or the gesture. *At the house*. Those were the only words that circled around my head. Faster and faster. *At the house, at the house, at the house*. Like race cars speeding at every pass. My heart pounded. *At the house. At the house*. I dressed with yesterday's clothes, opened the door, and ran out. The word house didn't ring the same as it normally would – that house was a portal to evil places. I needed to get there. I needed to get to Angelene.

The parking space in front of my room was empty. My car wasn't there anymore. I was trying to counterbalance the waves of feelings with rational thoughts. *Nothing has happened; she could have left the place ten minutes ago. Just wait*. Wait. And that's what I did. But ten minutes waiting are ten years to a worried mind. I ran back to the room to check my phone. It wasn't there. I'd left it in my car. Together with my wallet.

Fuck.

I tripped and fell on my way to the lobby to ask for a cab. I didn't hurt myself, but my clothes got dirty from the mud. The guy in the lobby had a puffy face and red cheeks, a hat squeezed on to a balloon head. The nametag read, in washed out letters, IJ. I moved closer and said,

IJ. Hi. I need you to call me a cab.

Sure thing. What's the room number?

I don't remember. I checked the keys in my pocket. 112. I showed IJ.

Are you checking out?

No. Just a ride. Three miles from here.

You don't have a car? IJ said, while his sausage-like fingers were making clickety noises on a grey keyboard.

Yes. My friend has it.

I see. You don't have a card on file, do you?

No, I'm paying cash. Why?

System lets me call a cabbie only if we have a card on file. If you gimme one I'll call the car for ya.

I threw my hands up in the air. What kind of fucked-up system is this where you need a plastic card to do any shit?

IJ's face became all serious and he squinted his eyes, now two black dots on the red balloon. Sorry, sir, he said. No card, no cab. It's policy.

I checked my pockets, but all the money I had was in the wallet. I leaned on the counter and spoke to IJ. Listen, can I make a call to the cab company? They'll send a cab. I'll pay the driver cash.

You can do that, sir, IJ replied, and gave me the handle of the phone.

His sausages dialed the number for me. I spoke to the voice on the other end and gave the name of the motel. Ten minutes away from my cab. I reluctantly thanked IJ and waited outside, arms crossed over my chest to keep my heart from racing out. *They're still sisters*, I thought. *Nothing will happen*, I thought. Then I realized that I was taking for granted that Mal was there and that she and Angie would have already met up. I took a deep breath. No. She went back to the house. She got the watch. She's on her way back. Maybe I should just wait here. The parking lot was empty and quiet and the minutes were passing one by one like grains of sand. I could hear myself getting old, I could feel the time passing on my skin – what is getting old, but increasingly feeling one's own mortality, one's own final moment?

I heard a flapping sound and turned my eyes up. Two crows landed on the motel roof. They cawed *at me,* and kept on cawing. I heard more flapping and three, four more birds joined the others. Like a punch, an image from my dream came back, and now my heart was trying to get out through my throat. I had to swallow and breathe deeply several times. The birds were together on the roof, now more than a dozen. My head was spinning. I felt faint and nauseous. But I held my ground. My foot was tapping and I was shaking. Where the hell was my cab? And like a granted wish, a car materialized slowly in the parking lot, an old man behind the wheel.

You the man who called? the driver asked.

Yes, I replied, and went to open the door. It was closed. Can you please open it? I added.

The driver leaned out the window. He took a good look at me and my dirty clothes. You paying cash?

Yes, I replied.

He kept looking at me. Where you goin'?

A house. Three, four miles from here. Close by.

Four miles ain't that close. You wouldn't mind showing me the dough, would you?

I groaned. My hand dropped from the door handle and both arms lay at my sides, powerless. I looked at him and said,

I have money, but it's in my wallet. And my wallet is in my car. Which is at the house I have to get to.

The driver's head snapped back into the cab like a turtle into his shell. Sorry, he said. No money, no service, pal.

Come on, I said. Please. I swear I have the money there. I'll pay you double.

His eyes looked at mine. He wasn't sure. Double, you say?

Yes. Yes. It's extremely important I reach that house.

He grabbed his chin and sat there, thinking. I felt confident I could convince him to get me to the house. After all, it was a short drive for him. He didn't speak for ten seconds or so. I heard a bell that signaled the lobby door. Voices coming out. Coming closer. A female one said, Excuse me, is that your cab?

I turned and saw her. A whale-like woman in a flowery dress that could have served as a bow-window drape.

Yes, ma'am. This is my cab.

From inside the cab the driver said, It ain't yet. Where you goin, ma'am?

The airport.

Come on in, the driver said.

What? No, wait! That's *my* cab! I shouted, both to the driver and the whale.

Ain't yours, man. The lady looks in better shape than you. Then he added Economically speaking, that is.

He got out of the cab, opened the trunk and helped the whale settle her luggage in, and then rushed around to the driver's seat and closed the door. The whale woman grinned at me, and with much trouble and sighing and squashing got into the cab. I watched, helpless, and when the cab slid away all the crows were still there, looking at me and cawing with their beaks open.

I took a small stone from the lot and threw it at them. Some of them flew away just enough to avoid the impact and then hopped back again, cawing uninterruptedly at my murder attempt.

A murder of crows. Again, I tried to rationalize. She'll be back. She'll be back. I went into my room. The digital clock spelled 8:30. I sat on the bed.

At 9:15 the ominous feeling wasn't just a feeling anymore, but everything that my head could think and contain. At 9:17 I was out of my room. I was going to walk to the house. After a couple hundred yards I saw the parking lot of a fast-food chain. The lot was empty, apart from an old motorcycle. I went up to it. I'd never driven one. I sat on it and fiddled with my right hand to find a lever to turn. I found it and turned it, using the pedal to turn it on. The engine came to life and blasted in the air. In the rearview mirror, I saw crows flying away from the motel, dark spots in the sky.

I turned the right handle and was on the road to the house.

When I pulled into the driveway my heart skipped a beat, but then recovered it, together with a thousand more. My car was there. But there was another car parked in front of it. I turned the engine off early enough that it wouldn't be heard approaching the house. The adrenaline started filling my system, and all my head spins were gone. I parked the bike behind a shed on the left side of the house. The shed was old and decaying. I tried to peer in to check its contents, but it was too dark. When I tried the door the wood cracked and the door swung open. The only thing in there resembling a weapon was a rusty hammer. I took it. From the shed I moved to the side of the house. The windows were high, but not so high that I couldn't see inside. I peeked in, but didn't see anyone.

The basement. Of course; they were in the basement. Mallory was here. The dream image of the two girls, dead, started running on loop in my mind. I moved quickly to reach the front door. With the hammer in my right hand, I slowly opened the door. Without widening it too much, I asked, Angie? but received no answer. I sidled in and closed the door behind me.

Trying to keep my back against the walls, I scanned the room. On the coffee table I saw that the watch was still there. Angie didn't take it. She didn't have time. I put it in my pocket. As a reflex, I looked around again to see if there was any trace of Neil.

Nothing.

I went to the basement door. I opened it. The stairs were unfolding into the darkness. I thought no one would be there in the dark. I flipped the switch and descended far enough to take a look. The basement was exactly as we left it. I turned the light off and was in the living room again. After I closed the basement door I finally heard a noise, and my muscles contracted and gripped the hammer tighter. Muffled voices. Upstairs. Without loosening my grip on the hammer, I started going up, step by step, carefully avoiding making any sound. When I reached the first floor, I could figure out which room the voices were coming from. Angie and Mal. They were talking, and from the sound of it neither one was raising the tone of the conversation. Maybe things were figuring themselves out, I thought, and relaxed my grip on the hammer a bit. I moved towards the voices in the room at the far end of the house.

The door was open. Like distorted mirrors of each other, Angelene and Mallory were standing there with their arms crossed. When they heard my steps, they turned at the same moment.

Louis, they said in unison.

twenty-three

Are you okay? I asked Angie.

Yes, she replied flatly, her arms crossed tight and her face cold and distant.

I turned towards Mallory. You better stop whatever is you're doing, I said. She smiled, but the expression her face made didn't transmit any feeling. Her mouth was just an open wound of nothingness. She moved one step closer to her sister. She put an arm around her shoulder, and to my surprise Angie didn't reject it. I raised my eyebrows and tightened my grip on the hammer again.

Mallory spoke. You think you could deceive us?

Me? What are you talking about? Angie, move away. She's dangerous.

Angie didn't move.

I'm dangerous? Cut the crap, Lou. You're lucky I didn't call the police. And I told Angie everything. She knows now. Mal's voice was sneaking up my spine like a snake climbing a tree.

What game are you playing, witch? I said.

Angie uncrossed her arms and pointed a finger at me. You lied to me, she said, her voice breaking. I trusted you, and you lied to my face!

All the spinning came back to my head at once and I felt a heavy weight on my shoulders. Gravity pressed me forward, and all the air I had in my body rushed itself out in a big sigh.

Alright, I said. What the hell are we talking about?

I told her. I told her how we met. What you *did*, said Mallory.

And what is it that I did? Stab myself? I said, pointing at my gut.

No. I did that, Mal said. But only because you raped me.

My hand let go of the hammer. My blood rushed down to my feet, passing through my knees, and then bounced and rushed back up to my brain. What the fuck are you saying?

Angie looked down.

Mal hissed at me. That you *raped* me, you bastard! That's why I stabbed you. And you're lucky I didn't go to the police. I was scared of you and your crazy psycho-stories.

I took a step back to lean on the wall. You're insane, I said to Mal. You're definitely, utterly, and completely insane.

Am I? Are you sure it isn't you? Do you still see your dead friend? Or the Grim Reaper himself?

You *saw* my friend! So you fucking said! You told me you could help! You fucking stabbed me! Words were being slung out of my mouth like arrows, but Mal seemed shielded.

I played along, Mal said. I was scared. Her voice filled with little high-pitched changes. And then like a real psycho you went to all those lengths to find my sister and lure her into your—her hands now waving in the air restlessly—your crazy world of spirits.

I looked at Angie. Don't believe her, I said. Don't believe a word. I did not lie.

Angie started to shake her head. I could see tears pushing against the invisible wall of will that resides in the eyes. She didn't answer. I could see her sorrow, the endless hole of abandonment swallowing her up again. I needed to counterattack, so I turned to Mal and asked,

How come you stabbed me in my apartment, then? How come you were far away from your house, in another city, with me? This doesn't add up, does it?

Mal grinned coldly. That's your word against mine, isn't it? For all we know you could tell any story. She tightened her arm around her sister, who smiled slightly and put a hand on Mal's arm.

Truth is a phone call away, I said. Let's just take the phone and call the hospital. They can confirm the date and time of my admission.

Mal removed her arm from her sister's shoulder and took a step towards me. Then why didn't you call the police, Lou?

I smirked. I thought, if that's the game you want to play, let's play. I took a step towards Mal. What if I did?

Angie—her face now red and streaked by tears—spoke. You told me you didn't.

That's because I didn't think you would have helped me, I said.

Then you lied to me. She crossed her arms again, and a world fell between us. She looked me directly in the eyes—that profound gaze that made my heart tremble and my body shiver. I felt defenseless.

No. No, I didn't, I said. I didn't lie to you. I wouldn't want to. I didn't call the police. I'm sorry.

Why? Angie asked.

Mal was watching us, contempt on her face.

Because I can promise on my dead friend that everything I said is true. Or true to me. Angie, you said it's the experience that's real. Well, everything was real to *me*. Neil dying was real. His ghost was real. And I thought your sister really wanted to help, before she stabbed me. And she told me she could perceive Neil, *see* him. And I believed that too.

My voice was calm, albeit the rushing pace of my thoughts and heart. I looked at Mal and said, Then she betrayed me and stabbed me for her own interests, and pointed my finger towards her. She spoke,

And what would my interests be?

You want to perform Lord knows what fucked-up ritual, based on your mother's research. You want to bring back—and I don't know how or why—your father. And from what Angie told me, you should think twice about it.

Mal put a hand over her mouth. Then started laughing. It was a giggle at first, but opened out into a loud hiccup of laughter. That's what you think I wanted to do? Bring my father back? What am I, *crazy?*

Angie wrinkled her forehead and looked at her sister. She licked away tears from her lips and then said You did perform all sorts of things with Mom, Mal. And last time I was here, you were talking about a blood ritual.

Mal sighed and said That's true, my sister. But I was in pain and so were you. Everyone reacts to sorrow in their own way. She moved towards Angie to hug her.

Don't you dare touch her, I said firmly.

What?

Don't you touch her. You might fool her, but I'm not falling for it.

I think I can say my sister believes *me*, and not you. Mal's mellifluous voice was silk on the ears. And if I asked you to confess that you had sex with me, you wouldn't be able to say that *that* was a lie. Am I right?

I saw Angie's face change shape again. Her mouth opened slightly and her eyes widened. I could see her shoulders dropping in disappointment and her cheeks losing color. I bit my lip and swung to the right and said,

Yes, I slept with you, but that's irrelevant.

Irrelevant? Angie blurted out. Irrelevant? You knock on my door and come into my house. You swear to tell me the truth and instead of telling me that you slept with my sister, you tell me tales of ghosts and who knows what else. Then we get here and what do you do? You force yourself on me.

Her words were sharp and every single one was an open cut in my heart. She continued, red in her face, anger taking over, burning coal of despair,

You tried to, to, to *fuck* me! Her hands were pointing at me and moving in the air, and if they weren't attached to her arms they would have flown someplace against the wall.

I was alone and in pain and I fell on you because I drank too much, I said with the most stupid and plain intonation.

But you weren't alone, or in pain, when we were on the road!

I didn't want you to get the wrong idea about me.

The wrong idea? The true idea!

I stood there, silent. Mal was keeping her smile halfway hidden. She was enjoying the show.

You should go, Angie said.

What?

Go. Take your fucking cesspool of a car and go. I don't wanna see you ever again. Ever. If you ever come close to me, I'll call the police.

Angie said this while moving towards her sister, who welcomed her with open arms. The movement revealed Mal's neck and what was there.

Hanging by a light thread, the golden necklace that I saw in Mal's room. Instinctively I reached into my pocket and touched Neil's watch.

In that moment I realized, with a clarity that had failed me so far, that Mal *needed* the necklace for whatever it was she wanted to do. With her words she was mixing truth and lies to deceive me and her sister, so she could go on with her plan. I mentally tried to put together the puzzle pieces. Mal approaching me and luring me into her bedroom. Probably just to have an alibi if she got caught after stabbing me. Why didn't she kill me then? She might have needed something more to complete the ritual. Maybe just more time. If she really wanted to bring her father back she needed a connection with me—my blood!—and a connection with her father: the necklace! She needed me alive. D warned me about it. That's why she was here. She was never far away. She probably followed me all the time and just waited for the right moment. Yes! But if the ritual was what we'd read in the notebooks, she needed more blood. And she couldn't take it from me if she needed me alive.

All these thoughts took place in a fraction of a second. I needed to have Angie on my side. The only move I had was to upset Mal and force her to reveal her true intentions. Mal and Angie were standing very close to each other. I took the watch out of my pocket and weighed it in my hand. I looked at the window. It was an old one, one thin pane of yellowed glass. I drew my arm back and then threw with all my strength. The watch flew five yards and broke the window with a crash. Mal and Angie jumped and turned to the window. With them distracted, I ran towards Mal and with one hand I grabbed the necklace and ripped it from her neck. The thread broke immediately and she put her hands to her throat. I had the necklace! I jumped back and fell on the ground and hid the hammer with my body.

You! You son of a bitch. Give it back to me, Mal screamed.

Why? Why's that thing so important? Why do you need it?, I replied.

You give it back to me!
I don't think so.

With a swift movement, I laid the necklace on the floor and took the hammer and started banging on it. The first blow made the little stone fly out and crushed the external part. I was just landing the second blow when I heard a small sound like a *pop!* and when I looked at my chest, on the left side there was a little hole in my t-shirt and I felt a stinging sensation on my skin, like an insect bite, and put my hand to it. It started to burn and the stinging started spreading. It reminded me of the stabbing, but it was a more profound sensation, with burning all around it. A dark spot painted itself on the dirty white t-shirt like a red rose blooming, and I raised my head and finally saw that Mal had a small handgun pointed at me. Angie's face was pale and her hands were keeping her mouth from screaming. I had no words to say. I let go of the hammer, and balancing with my free hand on my knees, I started standing up while the pain took control of my body.

Mal kept the gun pointed at me. Step aside, she said. I did as instructed and moved out of her way. My field of vision became smaller and I felt the warmth slipping out of my body and the room got painted in a darker shade and a thin mist was covering my eyes and everything reminded me of when I first met D. And as Mallory kneeled to grab the necklace I saw him again. *Death, my Death.* And this time the end wasn't despair and desolation, it wasn't darkness and horror; the end was mellow and sweet, a lullaby of thorns, a flight of the soul, birds chanting on the eternal trees, sunshine smiling on the flesh; the end wasn't the end.

D was standing there behind Mal, looking at me with a sardonic smile on his face. He probably spoke, but I could hear no words, as a ringing sound was filling my ears. Mal was still on the ground with the gun arm extended towards me, looking for the stone and muttering something to herself. Angie was petrified. D started walking towards me and now, like magic and without tequila, I could see Neil. And from the window a little crow came in, and within the space of two hops he was standing tall next to D. This is it, I thought. And all the poems I had running in my blood finally came back to my mind, all at once, their meaning revealed;

Dead men naked they shall be one.

Though they go mad they shall be sane.

And Death shall have no dominion.

I gathered what strength I had and took a jump at Mal and she saw me coming and jumped backwards and I heard another *pop!* and Angie's voice screaming No! but it didn't matter because I reached Mal and she fell back and her head thumped hard on the floor and she was lying there with her eyes closed and we were both on the floor, shivering. I could see the movement of her chest. All around me the room was getting darker and my eyes were closing and the last thing I saw was Angie with her hands on her belly and dark red flowers of blood and next to her - next to her a marvelous red-headed woman, looking at her. And Angie saw her and I swear she looked at me and at Neil and the Crow and D and I thought *She finally sees everything I see and knows everything I know* and then I saw her dropping to her knees and then leaning with her back against the wall just below the window and her face was covered in tears and her hands were pressing her belly and the sun came in from the window and all I could see was her shadow; she was a being of Beauty.

There is grass all around me. Purple grass. I'm on top of a hill in the middle of my City. I'm sitting on a bench, black and made of stone. I recognize some of the painted houses, but all the colors seem off. The wind is caressing the trees with a hissing, calming noise. If this is heaven or hell, I can't tell. I look around and far away. The sea before me is white as milk and the sky bright orange. In the cracks of the clouds I see giant whale-women, their skin adorned by flowers, swimming and pushing more white clouds with their breath. I stare at the picture unfolding before my eyes: the most accurate representation of the City I've ever seen.

But this time I know. This time is different. This time,

I know I'm dreaming.

I look around. I might very well be dead, I say to myself. Death is a walk in your dreams. And next to me, sitting on the bench, is Neil. He's wearing a black suit with a black shirt. I can't figure out if he's a projection of my will, a manifestation of my brain chemistry, or the soul of the man I knew. It doesn't really matter.

Five more minutes, he says.

I keep silent, staring at the flying whales.

After the five minutes have passed, we stand up together. And the first thing we do is hug, because you can believe in souls and the afterlife but arms don't lie when you put them around the people you love. I'd never told him that I love him. I don't say it now and it doesn't matter because I know he feels it; he knows it. But I feel regret for the times I could have said it.

Where are you? I ask.

I am *not* anymore, he replies.

How does it feel?

It doesn't.

As clear as the words sounded to me then, so cloudy they seem, now that I repeat them:

Death is a human concept. You create time because that's the way you live the experience. Once you're out of it, there's no time; there is no existence. You'll understand. Now we have to go.

We walk down the hill and out of the park and past a small pond. Fish are circling in an endless merry-go-round, and at every pass they make a sound like tiny drums. We keep walking until we are out of the City completely, and suddenly we're on a raft in the middle of the white sea. Neil looks at me and says, You can find them.

I walk towards the end of the raft, but with every step I take the raft grows bigger and bigger, like an endless gangway. I walk and walk. Eventually Neil says, I always wanted to fly, and a pair of wings rip out of his shoulders, big and white. He grabs me and flaps once, twice, until we're high in the sky that now is a deep blue. Looking down, the raft looks like a toy. We're flying around Mal and Angie's house and the raft is a toy in a pond. We land just by it. We look at each other and without saying a word we enter the house.

Everything is decaying. The place is a living organism, and if I fix my eyes on a single point the walls seem to breathe on their own. Shadows are moving around, as though the sun is rising and falling every few seconds. We shout Hello? but nothing and no one answers and we hear a voice from upstairs. We walk up the stairs and we skip all the rooms until we reach the last one on the right. The room where Mal shot me.

The room has glass walls, and I see Mal and Angie playing outside on the lawn. They're dressed as little girls even though they're grown-ups. When I turn, a woman is standing in the middle of the room. She is beautiful, pale and distant. I recognize her from the pictures; she is the girls' mother. She doesn't acknowledge our presence.

Hello, I say.

She doesn't reply.

Hello?

She slowly brings her eyes to me.

Hi. I'm Louis. I raise my hand in greeting.

She smiles faintly.

I believe Mal and Angie are outside, I say, and point towards the two girls on the lawn. Neil is in a black suit, his wonderful white wings gone.

What's your name? I ask the woman.

She glides towards me.

Can you understand me? I say.

She nods. She takes her face in her hands and says, Eliza.

Your name is Eliza, I repeat.

She nods.

Are Angie and Mal your daughters? I ask.

She nods again. They're outside. They're playing, she says.

I take a step closer. They're outside and not outside. I say, I believe this is a dream. I don't know if you're a projection of the dream or something else entirely.

She doesn't move or speak.

Do you remember your girls? I ask.

She moves her eyes to the ceiling. Yes, she says. I remember them.

As she says so, I look outside. The two girls have their faces turned towards us, and as soon as they see us they start running towards the door.

They're coming, Neil says.

Yes.

The walls now change again, becoming normal, grey. The room looks like a normal room. The steps of the girls on the stairs resonate through the house, through the bones. Then silence. And nothing happens for what feels like an eternity, until Mal's voice breaks it,

Lou? I know you're in there. We saw you. Come out and you'll be fine.

Neil and I look at each other. We're not alone, I say.

Eliza is here, Neil says.

Leave her out, the door, with Mal's voice, says.

You really care about her, don't you? Neil asks.

The door doesn't answer.

Well, if you don't answer, I think I'll just take her with me.

With a big swing the door opens, and it reveals a hallway, again different from the original, real one. Mal and Angie are there. Their bodies are without any clothes and I realize we are all naked, but this doesn't bother us. Angie leaps into the room and scrambles to hug her mother, who returns the gesture with open arms. Then Eliza says Who are you? – and Angie moves her face away from her mother's chest. She says, Mom, it's me. It's Angie. Eliza looks at the big green eyes, almost seeing them for the first time again. Mal is still at the door, her face red and her eyes tearing up.

They broke it! Mal shouts eventually. They broke the necklace, and now look! Mom, are you okay? Mom!

Mal runs towards her mother and Eliza lets go of Angie and runs for the door. The room has four concrete walls, tall as skyscrapers, without a roof and no door to leave through.

Mal looks at me and Neil and says,

You. This is your fault! I would have brought her back! Now it's all useless, useless!

Angie looks at her sister, puzzled, and says, Bring her back?

Yes. Yes! Do you really think I wanted to bring back that pig of a father? Come on! All I wanted was to have Mom back. Have her beauty back. Her face back and her time back and her kisses back. Dad died and we were free and all she could do was try to get him back! And I hated it. But I helped her, because at least we were close, together! I would have never believed it. I thought it was her way of dealing with it. Dealing with loss. With Death. I humored her. But then—she paused, her voice breaking, her breath becoming intense, and the walls of the room breathing with her, inside and outside— Then something worked. It worked, do you understand?

Neil moves close to Eliza. She is now quiet, distant. The same state in which we found her.

How did you find her? Angie asks, directly to me.

She was here. She's been here all the time. If I were to bet, I'd guess Mal bound your mother to the necklace.

Mal's face becomes red, a face of anger. Yes! She shouted. That's it! I taught you well! Keep a connection with the dead. That's what I did! I could have brought her back!

Did you, Angie says, pausing, did you keep her here? The whole time?

Mal doesn't answer. Her face is distorting and her breathing affects her whole body, like she is breathing not from her mouth but from her skin. I look up as a ceiling appears, but it is no relief. The cement starts filling with cracks and crumbling. The walls are coming down flake after flake, like a gray snowstorm, and everything is moving rhythmically in and out, synchronized to Mal's breathing.

You did, Angie says.

And everything breaks into a million pieces and I close my eyes and fall. When I open them I'm on a raft again, but the sea is no longer white, it's black as tar. I look in the dark waters and I see hundreds, thousands, millions of fish swimming and shining in silvery shades, the water is crawling with them. One jumps right in front of my eyes and I see its mouth. And its white teeth. And its white eyes. And even in the *dreamworld,* it stings me in the heart to understand that these things are not fish.

Humans.

What's left of them.

This is the place of the dead, the common grave, the pit of souls, the *Shéol.*

Filled with all the souls that the living couldn't let go.

The raft dances up and down on the thick black waters. Up to the horizon stretches the dark sea and the dark clouds. Angie shrieks and her hands go to her face. I work to keep my balance. Everyone on the raft looks scared. The clouds gather in a thick foam directly above our heads.

Is that true? Angie shouts at her sister. You have to tell me!

I saved her, Mal replies. I saved her while you were away. That's what I did.

You didn't save her, Neil says. His eyes look quickly around the raft, at all those souls that never got away. I can feel his distress when he says, You condemned her to a worse fate.

Mal's face turns long and serious, and for a moment I believe she is about to cry, but a menacing laugh cracks from her mouth as she takes Eliza by the hand.

You don't understand, she says. The things we discovered, the things we saw together, Mom and I. Whatever Mom was doing to bring Dad back was just the beginning. I can avoid this; I can avoid her death. Reverse it! Mal pronounces, the whites of her eyes crazed by a red web, and continues, Yes, I needed blood, but the blood of a living person. Someone I was connected to. And yes, I followed Louis around, because he was my sacrificial lamb, the blood to bathe in to complete the ritual. I just needed a host for Mom.

Angie crumples to her knees. Her face is pale and her eyes are big and I can see her heart has cracked. She has no words to throw against her sister. She has no words for the craziness that takes place in the heart when the people you love are gone. Still crouching, she says,

That's not Mom. Not anymore.

Mal smiles, and keeping her mother's shade next to her says slowly, My dear sister. We'll see. You probably won't. That's where the ritual will take place, the place between dream and death. And we have all the ingredients; Louis here is bleeding away. And your body will be a perfect host.

Mal's face is calm. Angie has no power or will to counter anything that is happening. She is lost, as lost as her mother. Her strength brought her here, but now it is the time of revelations.

All around us, shells of human beings are dancing in the dark fluid. I am petrified. So I don't react when Neil jumps straight at Mal.

Mal is quick enough to slide to the side and Neil loses his balance. I see his terror when he falls in the water, like a drop in the sea. I throw myself down and reach out to help him. I put my arm in the water, calling his name. The water is thick and slimy and cloudy and it feels like I'm drowning my hands in a pool of liquid night. My arms move just beneath the surface, grasping and grabbing and feeling soft, horrible things all around. I can't get a grip on Neil, and I see him emerge for a moment and then drift away. Eight, nine, ten feet away from the raft, and he's lost in the strange sea. The last thing I see are his eyes, scared not of leaving, but of staying where he no longer belongs.

The light is now darker and darker and the clouds are coming down. Then a bird comes, gliding down just above the water. It extends its legs and grabs something and takes it into the air like a predator. I look around and there is another one falling from the dark sky into the water and up again with its prey.

But those are not birds; those above are not clouds.

One for every man or woman, thousands of millions of beings are the clouds above.

My arm is stuck in the water and I can't tear my eyes away from this *wild hunt*. Some of the beings in the water are jumping towards their death and they fly together like hummingbirds, quickly vanishing. Some of the deaths have to hover and even submerge until their mate will come with them, screaming and kicking. And lost in the marvelous tragedy I finally feel a hand grabbing my wrist, but it's not Neil's, and I am pulled down, down into the water. The dark figure that pulls me climbs onto the raft and it is human in shape, but has the smell of a wild beast. It looks at Mal and Angie and a low growl comes from its chest. I fight to stay afloat and my mouth screams and bites and my legs kick, but the tar is heavy and with every second I am drowning deeper down. With a frantic kick of my legs, I rise out of the water enough to see and hear Angie and Mal, together, say to the black figure,

Dad?

I do not feel. I do not hear. I do not see. I am none and none and all, the darkness of the soul, the last drop of light extinguished. I am terror and despair, I am happiness and hope. The skin and the water, the dark and the light, and me in the middle, a membrane, the balance of it all.

I am floating in the dark. I have no thoughts passing through my mind. I am all and nothing, swallowed in the black. My last glimpse of a thought is that soon D will have to come down here and take me away with him. And while I am expecting his hands to grab me, it still comes as a surprise when I feel a touch. A small one at first, growing in intensity, like hands trying to grab hold of me. I come back to my senses and kick up, and the hands reach out on me until my eyes are out of the dark, and I see that it isn't D pulling me up but Eliza. The dark figure is holding the two girls cornered on the side of the raft. They are helpless and frightened. I put my hands on the raft and shout, and the dark figure turns towards me and the only thing I see is the white teeth and the white eyes but no fear finds a place in my heart, and when I am ready to charge at it I see a quick movement behind it.

Angelene. Standing tall behind the black figure. Without hesitation she charges at it and her body weight is enough to throw it off balance, as they fall over the side of the raft, into the endless sea. Mal leaps towards her mother, while I jump again into the water to help Angelene. The water is now clear and I see the black figure falling down, deep down, facing a death that never was explored during his life, heavy with sins and unable to resurface.

Angie is close to me, floating lightly on the water, her eyes closed: senseless. I swim to her as the water gets lighter and grab her and push her up onto the raft where Mal is caressing her mother, telling her that now is the right moment, now is the time, but Eliza is crying. She opens her mouth and in between sighs I hear the words, *Let me go. Let me go. Let me go.*

It is a prayer and a scream that enters my soul and explodes outwards in a million needles. Let me go, she says again, and this time Mal hears it.

And she says,

No. No, I will never let you go. I cannot let you go.

Angie is on the raft. She is still breathing. I pull myself up. Eliza is on her knees crying and Mal is standing there. Mal helps her mother to stand, but I hear a swooshing sound and an ancient scream and then I see it again.

The crow is flying down on us. It stands on the raft and its eyes are fierce and this time it doesn't speak. From its huge foot it releases something.

Neil. And his face is serene and his eyes are calm.

Mal is distracted by the Crow, and Eliza stands up swiftly and leaps into the water, but she doesn't manage to even ripple the surface as a light wind carries her up and above the clouds and she disappears in a gentle breeze, with the same grace by which she lived. When Mal realizes her mother is gone forever she lets out a scream so loud that the raft rocks and waves expand out from it. Without breaking her war cry she looks at me and jumps to attack.

But she never reaches me.

Neil puts himself in the middle and throws his arms around her to hold her tight. And she screams and shouts and growls. Neil looks at me and says, Go, now!, so I kneel to take Angie in my arms as she is still unconscious and she won't wake up. And from the clouds I notice, beautiful and shiny, the woman with the red hair, wearing nothing this time but a piteous smile. And I know she is coming for Angie. I scream No! and start shaking Angie while Neil keeps Mal powerless in his arms. And the clouds open suddenly and there I see him. My Death is here. And with Angie in my arms I try to jump and at the same moment Death takes me by the hand and I am not afraid.

And Neil lets go of Mal and leaps on to the head of the giant Crow and flies away, smiling at me.

Mal is alone with the red-haired woman. As I fly away I see the woman hugging her.

And I'm one with the white clouds.

twenty-four

Are we fallen angels who didn't want to believe that nothing is nothing and so were born to lose our loved ones and dear friends one by one and finally our own life, to see it proved?

The first thing I noticed was my heart. The sudden surprise of feeling it beat, still.

Alive. I was alive.

My body ached everywhere. I was cold. I opened my eyes and it took me a moment to adjust to the light of the room. I couldn't remember exactly what had happened, and as I was lying on the floor I moved my hands to support me and the pain hit me strong in the left side of my chest and my hands slid on some liquid on the floor and I fell again. Then I remembered flashes from the wild dream and I slowly realized that I was lying in a pool of blood. Carefully, to avoid pain, I raised myself up and looked around, my heart offering everything it had.

Leaning against the window, with light beaming from behind, sat Angie in a sea of blood. Her face was inclined to the right and the white curtains fell on her hair and her figure, wrapping her. Her hands were on her belly.

The floor was covered in blood. On my right was Mal, unconscious from the hit to the head. While moving towards Angie I remembered that I'd jumped at Mal. I remembered the bang of the gun and Angie falling. I reached out towards her, uncaring of the pain, but my hands only confirmed what my heart was pounding to tell me.

Angie lay there, as beautiful in death as she was in life. I closed her eyes with my hands, leaving a streak of blood on her lovely face, and I poured my soul from my eyes and cried.

I lay there hugging her for an infinite amount of time, but my body wasn't warm enough to bring her back. And the prayers to the gods were useless and nothing out of this world showed up to comfort me or show me the way. As the wind raised its cry outside, I listened to it as it passed through the field of daisies that I could see through the window. And the sun broke down and everything was dark. And there was Mal's body, unconscious, but breathing.

I stood up and kissed Angie on her forehead. Took the gun from Mal's hand and put it in the back of my pants. Walked into the hallway and found the bathroom. Turned on the faucet. The water was yellowish; I drank a good amount of it. I opened the cabinet and found some stale pills; painkillers. I opened the cap, and without caring if they were expired, swallowed a handful of them. I moved to the shower. It wasn't working.

It was hard to get my t-shirt off. I looked at myself in the mirror. On the edge of my chest I saw the bullet wound. An almost-perfect round hole. There were filaments of cotton from the t-shirt and the wound was dark with crusted blood. I turned around so I could see the other side in the mirror. An irregular hole, dirty with dried-up blood. The bullet went in and out. I wasn't bleeding. Not anymore.

I turned on the faucet again and let the water run until it became clearer in color. I drank more of it and my stomach started groaning. I pressed one hand on the faucet to direct the stream at the wound and cleaned it as best I could. It hurt, but that pain was nothing compared to what my heart was feeling. Then I found and opened a pack of gauze, and applied it loosely on both sides of my chest. There was some tape that I used to keep the bandages in place. I went back into the bedroom and opened the closet and took a shirt. I buttoned it while looking at Angie and Mal.

Then I sat on the chair and cried.

She was still unconscious. I didn't call the police. For some reason I couldn't explain, I didn't manage to hate her. I carefully half-carried, half-dragged her body down the stairs and into the car. She didn't wake up. On the grass I saw pieces of glass and looked up. I was right under the broken window. I looked around and saw Neil's watch. I took it, put it in my pocket, and went back into the house.

Upstairs, Angelene's body was a dark spot against the wall. I crouched and kissed her eyes and stood up again.

And left her to the indifferent stars above.

Two hours down the road I checked into a motel. The desert sand was dancing in the wind all around me. I got a room on the ground floor with access to the lot and two separate beds. When I got the keys I went back to my car and looked around to see if anyone was watching. Then I opened the door, and with great effort I got her out and carefully placed her on the first bed. She was still unconscious or asleep or something else entirely, her original soul lost someplace I've touched or dreamed.

I closed the door and went out and got some food from the vending machines and some ice to put on my wound. It burned. And it smelled bad. The ice helped to ease the pain a little. Meanwhile, I watched her sleeping. Her body was moving up and down, gently and rhythmically, unaware of the world outside. I sort of sat and sort of lay on the bed, and even if I wanted to cry there were no more tears. So I stayed there in the dark with my hands on my chest, and after a million breaths I fell asleep into a dream with no dreams.

The blessed oblivion lasted all night and part of the next day. When I opened my eyes reality hit me hard. On the bed next to mine her body was quiet and beautiful. In her sleep, they were the same. She could have never woken up again, forever suspended. I thought of Neil for a moment. I reached into my pocket and touched the rounded piece of metal of the watch. I got up, left the room, and entered the car. I drove west for a while until I saw a sign for a lake. I followed the track that ended at a small, white shore. I didn't want to bring the gun with me, as there were people around, so I opened the dashboard to leave it there. I saw Angelene's pack of cigarettes and her lighter. I took them out and put the gun in and walked to the water.

Calm and green.

I stood there contemplating everything and nothing for a while, and then I reached into my pocket to take out Neil's watch. I kissed it and threw it into the water and said farewell to my best friend.

Then I lit a cigarette and just held it in my hand and let it burn away.

I was back in the hotel at sundown with some food. I brought some extra in case she was awake. She wasn't. A part of me wanted to not be alone. I wished for Death to come. But as much as you can rejoice and make peace with your death, it's even more important to face your life. And at that exact moment I was facing myself, and her sleeping body.

I ate sparingly; I wasn't hungry. I checked the wound and it looked clean.

Healing.

I felt my forehead to check for fever and was relieved to find nothing was wrong.

I'd survived.

I turned on the TV to fill the air. I didn't pay attention until the news came on. In her childhood home the body of Angelene Day, profession exotic dancer, was found dead from a gunshot. First evidence suggested a fight gone bad, maybe a robbery, as no valuables were found in the house, even if it has indeed been uninhabited for a while. No suspects had yet been identified.

I killed the volume first and the TV immediately after.

She would have preferred just dancer, I said to myself.

They'd found her body, but they'd never find her soul.

The next morning I woke up early with the first ray of sunlight. Her body was still there, still breathing. I was still in bed when I heard a sound outside the room. *D? Is that you?* I said without thinking. I walked to the door and looked through the eyehole.

No one.

I opened the door and on the porch there was a small black crow. I felt blood rushing to my head and looked around to see Neil or D, but no one was there. The little crow didn't look scared and kept poking the small crumb on the ground with its beak. Then it looked inside the room and flew on to the bed where she was resting.

The crow turned its head to the side to take a look at her face. Then it turned its gaze upon me and back to her and touched her lips with its beak and flew away. I stayed at the door, watching the flying bird transform into a small black dot in the sky. The noise outside made me not hear that from inside another noise was coming—one of a person waking up after a long dream and learning how to use a body again—and I noticed it only when, paired with a cry, I heard my name from behind.

Louis?

I didn't turn. I stayed there, leaning on the door and looking up at the sky. Tears abruptly filled my eyes. And two arms hugged me from behind. And from skin to skin the souls transpired, and I had no doubts.

I turned. Her face was a cloth sewn with stars born during the dream of the endless. I sank my tears inside and my eyes into the emerald color of her exquisite ones.

And I kissed her on her lips for the first time.

And with that kiss I was born again.

thank you

Thank you for reading this book. I hope you liked it as much as I did while sharing in the stories of Lou, Neil, Mal, and Angelene. I'll miss them.

Louis had a knack for poetry, and that made telling his story a pleasure. We share a favorite poet, Dylan Thomas – I suggest you go read *Twenty-four years*, my favorite, together with *And Death Shall Have No Dominion*, Lou's favorite, which gave title to this book.

When I set out to write this story, I did it to explore my mortality, and the one of my loved ones, and if you will, of everyone else. *Dead Men Naked* did stay under my skin much longer after I finished writing it, and it did help me understand that *pain is temporary, love is eternal*.

I can't wait to hear what you think about it. Tell me here: dc@dariowrites.com or on IG and Twitter (@dariowrites).

Of course, I want to thank my wife, my family, and my friends – without them, I wouldn't be who I am. Special thanks to my first readers – Nico, Tom, Marisa, Staci, Kelly, Sarah, Austin – for their feedback during the early drafts. A huge thank you to my editors, Meredith Tennant and Alfonso Colasuonno, who took care of my writing like it was their baby.

Namaste.

Cork, Ireland, 2015-2017

ABOUT THE AUTHOR

DARIO CANNIZZARO is an Irish-Italian Writer, Poet, and Director. His stories, characterised by weird premises and poetic flights of fancy, have appeared in many literary magazines both in English and Italian. He lives in Cork, Ireland, and is currently working on his next novel and feature film.

When he's not making up stuff, he's probably reading books and comics, playing videogames, playing guitar and singing his heart out, or watching Sci-Fi stuff.

Made in the USA
Monee, IL
29 September 2021

78980939R10142